MURIEL
SPARK

THE PORTOBELLO ROAD
AND OTHER STORIES

PENGUIN BOOKS

PENGUIN BOOKS

Published by the Penguin Group. Penguin Books Ltd, 27 Wrights Lane, London
w8 5TZ, England. Penguin Books USA Inc., 375 Hudson Street, New York,
New York 10014, USA. Penguin Books Australia Ltd, Ringwood, Victoria,
Australia. Penguin Books Canada Ltd, 10 Alcorn Avenue, Toronto, Ontario,
Canada M4V 3B2. Penguin Books (NZ) Ltd, 182–190 Wairau Road, Auckland 10,
New Zealand · Penguin Books Ltd, Registered Offices: Harmondsworth,
Middlesex, England · **These stories are taken from** *The Collected Stories
of Muriel Spark*, **published by Penguin Books in 1994.** This edition pub-
lished 1995 · Copyright © Muriel Spark, 1958, 1961. Copyright © Copyright
Administration, 1985. All rights reserved · Typeset by Datix International
Limited, Bungay, Suffolk. Printed in England by Clays Ltd, St Ives plc · Except in
the United States of America, this book is sold subject to the condition that it
shall not, by way of trade or otherwise, be lent, re-sold, hired out, or otherwise
circulated without the publisher's prior consent in any form of binding or cover
other than that in which it is published and without a similar condition including
this condition being imposed on the subsequent purchaser · 10 9 8 7 6 5 4 3 2 1

CONTENTS

The Portobello Road   1

Bang-bang You're Dead   29

The Seraph and the Zambesi   64

The Dragon   74

The Portobello Road

One day in my young youth at high summer, lolling with my lovely companions upon a haystack, I found a needle. Already and privately for some years I had been guessing that I was set apart from the common run, but this of the needle attested the fact to my whole public: George, Kathleen and Skinny. I sucked my thumb, for when I had thrust my idle hand deep into the hay, the thumb was where the needle had stuck.

When everyone had recovered George said, 'She put in her thumb and pulled out a plum.' Then away we were into our merciless hacking-hecking laughter again.

The needle had gone fairly deep into the thumby cushion and a small red river flowed and spread from this tiny puncture. So that nothing of our joy should lag, George put in quickly,

'Mind your bloody thumb on my shirt.'

Then hac-hec-hoo, we shrieked into the hot Borderland afternoon. Really I should not care to be so young of heart again. That is my thought every time I turn over my old papers and come across the photograph. Skinny, Kathleen and myself are in the photo atop the haystack. Skinny had just finished analysing the inwards of my find.

'It couldn't have been done by brains. You haven't much brains but you're a lucky wee thing.'

Everyone agreed that the needle betokened extraordinary luck. As it was becoming a serious conversation, George said,

'I'll take a photo.'

I wrapped my hanky round my thumb and got myself organized. George pointed up from his camera and shouted,

'Look, there's a mouse!'

Kathleen screamed and I screamed although I think we knew there was no mouse. But this gave us an extra session of squalling hee-hoos. Finally we three composed ourselves for George's picture. We looked lovely and it was a great day at the time, but I would not care for it all over again. From that day I was known as Needle.

One Saturday in recent years I was mooching down the Portobello Road, threading among the crowds of marketers on the narrow pavement when I saw a woman. She had a haggard, careworn, wealthy look, thin but for the breasts forced-up high like a pigeon's. I had not seen her for nearly five years. How changed she was! But I recognized Kathleen, my friend; her features had already begun to sink and protrude in the way that mouths and noses do in people destined always to be old for their years. When I had last seen her, nearly five years ago, Kathleen, barely thirty, had said,

'I've lost all my looks, it's in the family. All the women are handsome as girls, but we go off early, we go brown and nosey.'

I stood silently among the people, watching. As you will see, I wasn't in a position to speak to Kathleen. I saw her shoving in her avid manner from stall to stall. She was always fond of antique jewellery and of bargains. I wondered that I had not seen her before in the Portobello Road on my Saturday morning ambles. Her long stiff-crooked fingers pounced to select a jade ring from amongst the jumble of brooches and pendants, onyx, moonstone and gold, set out on the stall.

'What do you think of this?' she said.

I saw then who was with her. I had been half-conscious of the huge man following several paces behind her, and now I noticed him.

'It looks all right,' he said. 'How much is it?'

'How much is it?' Kathleen asked the vendor.

I took a good look at this man accompanying Kathleen. It was her husband. The beard was unfamiliar, but I recognized beneath it his enormous mouth, the bright sensuous lips, the large brown eyes forever brimming with pathos.

It was not for me to speak to Kathleen, but I had a sudden inspiration which caused me to say quietly,

'Hallo, George.'

The giant of a man turned round to face the direction of my face. There were so many people – but at length he saw me.

'Hallo, George,' I said again.

Kathleen had started to haggle with the stall-owner, in her old way, over the price of the jade ring. George continued to stare at me, his big mouth slightly parted so that I could see a wide slit of red lips and white teeth between the fair grassy growths of beard and moustache.

'My God!' he said.

'What's the matter?' said Kathleen.

'Hallo, George!' I said again, quite loud this time, and cheerfully.

'Look!' said George. 'Look who's there, over beside the fruit stall.'

Kathleen looked but didn't see.

'Who is it?' she said impatiently.

'It's Needle,' he said. 'She said, "Hallo, George."'

'*Needle*,' said Kathleen. 'Who do you mean? You don't mean our old friend *Needle* who –'

'Yes. There she is. My God!'

He looked very ill, although when I had said, 'Hallo, George,' I had spoken friendly enough.

'I don't see anyone faintly resembling poor Needle,' said Kathleen looking at him. She was worried.

George pointed straight at me. 'Look *there*. I tell you that is Needle.'

'You're ill, George. Heavens, you must be seeing things. Come on home, Needle isn't there. You know as well as I do, Needle is dead.'

I must explain that I departed this life nearly five years ago. But I did not altogether depart this world. There were those odd things still to be done which one's executors can never do properly. Papers to be looked over, even after the executors have torn them up. Lots of business except, of course, on Sundays and Holidays of Obligation, plenty to take an interest in for the time being. I take my recreation on Saturday mornings. If it is a wet Saturday I wander up and down the substantial lanes of Woolworth's as I did when I was young and visible. There is a pleasurable spread of objects on the counters which I now perceive and exploit with a certain detachment, since it suits with my condition of life. Creams, toothpastes, combs and hankies, cotton gloves, flimsy flowering scarves, writing-paper and crayons, ice-cream cones and orangeade, screwdrivers, boxes of tacks, tins of paint, of glue, of marmalade; I always liked them but far more now that I have no need of any. When Saturdays are fine I go instead to the Portobello Road where formerly I would jaunt with Kathleen in our grown-up days. The barrow-loads do not change much, of apples and rayon vests in common blues and low-taste mauve, of silver plate, trays and teapots long since changed hands from the bygone citizens to dealers, from shops to the new flats and breakable homes, and then over to the barrow-stalls and the dealers again: Georgian spoons, rings, earrings of turquoise and opal set in the butterfly pattern of true-lovers' knots, patch-boxes with miniature paintings of ladies on ivory, snuff-boxes of silver with Scotch pebbles inset.

Sometimes as occasion arises on a Saturday morning, my friend Kathleen, who is a Catholic, has a Mass said for my soul, and then I am in attendance, as it were, at the church. But most Saturdays I take my delight among the solemn crowds with their aimless purposes, their eternal life not far away, who push past the counters and stalls, who handle, buy, steal, touch, desire and ogle the merchandise. I hear the tinkling tills, I hear the jangle of loose change and tongues and children wanting to hold and have.

That is how I came to be in the Portobello Road that Saturday morning when I saw George and Kathleen. I would not have spoken had I not been inspired to it. Indeed it's one of the things I can't do now – to speak out, unless inspired. And most extraordinary, on that morning as I spoke, a degree of visibility set in. I suppose from poor George's point of view it was like seeing a ghost when he saw me standing by the fruit barrow repeating in so friendly a manner, 'Hallo, George!'

We were bound for the south. When our education, what we could get of it from the north, was thought to be finished, one by one we were sent or sent for to London. John Skinner, whom we called Skinny, went to study more archaeology, George to join his uncle's tobacco farm, Kathleen to stay with her rich connections and to potter intermittently in the Mayfair hat shop which one of them owned. A little later I also went to London to 5 see life, for it was my ambition to write about life, which first I had to see.

'We four must stick together,' George said very often in that yearning way of his. He was always desperately afraid of neglect. We four looked likely to shift off in different directions and George did not trust the other three of us not to forget all about him. More and more as the time came for him to depart for his uncle's tobacco farm in Africa he said,

'We four must keep in touch.'

And before he left he told each of us anxiously,

'I'll write regularly, once a month. We must keep together for the sake of the old times.' He had three prints taken from the negative of that photo on the haystack, wrote on the back of them 'George took this the day that Needle found the needle' and gave us a copy each. I think we all wished he could become a bit more callous.

During my lifetime I was a drifter, nothing organized. It was difficult for my friends to follow the logic of my life. By the normal reckonings I should have come to starvation and ruin, which I never did. Of course, I did not live to write about life as I wanted to do. Possibly that is why I am inspired to do so now in these peculiar circumstances.

I taught in a private school in Kensington for almost three months, very small children. I didn't know what to do with them but I was kept fairly busy escorting incontinent little boys to the lavatory and telling the little girls to use their handkerchiefs. After that I lived a winter holiday in London on my small capital, and when that had run out I found a diamond bracelet in the cinema for which I received a reward of fifty pounds. When it was used up I got a job with a publicity man, writing speeches for absorbed industrialists, in which the dictionary of quotations came in very useful. So it went on. I got engaged to Skinny, but shortly after that I was left a small legacy, enough to keep me for six months. This somehow decided me that I didn't love Skinny so I gave him back the ring.

But it was through Skinny that I went to Africa. He was engaged with a party of researchers to investigate King Solomon's mines, that series of ancient workings ranging from the ancient port of Ophir, now called Beira, across Portuguese East Africa and Southern Rhodesia to the mighty jungle-city of Zimbabwe whose temple walls still stand by the approach to an ancient and sacred mountain, where the rubble of that civilization scatters itself over the surrounding Rhodesian waste. I accompanied the party as a sort of secretary. Skinny vouched for me, he paid my fare, he sympathized by his action with my inconsequential life although when he spoke of it he disapproved. A life like mine annoys most people; they go to their jobs every day, attend to things, give orders, pummel typewriters, and get two or three weeks off every year, and it vexes them to see someone else not bothering to do these things and yet getting away with it, not starving, being lucky as they call it. Skinny, when I had broken off our engagement, lectured me about this, but still he took me to Africa knowing I should probably leave his unit within a few months.

We were there a few weeks before we began inquiring for George, who was farming about four hundred miles away to the north. We had not told him of our plans.

'If we tell George to expect us in his part of the world he'll come rushing to pester us the first week. After all, we're going on business,' Skinny had said.

Before we left Kathleen told us, 'Give George my love and tell him not to send frantic cables every time I don't answer his letters right away. Tell him I'm busy in the hat shop and being presented. You would think he hadn't another friend in the world the way he carries on.'

We had settled first at Fort Victoria, our nearest place of access to the Zimbabwe ruins. There we made inquiries about George. It was clear he hadn't many friends. The older settlers were the most tolerant about the half-caste woman he was living with, as we found, but they were furious about his methods of raising tobacco which we learned were most unprofessional and in some mysterious way disloyal to the whites. We could never discover how it was that George's style of tobacco farming gave the blacks opinions about themselves, but that's what the older settlers claimed. The newer immigrants thought he was unsociable and, of course, his living with that nig made visiting impossible.

I must say I was myself a bit off-put by this news about the brown woman. I was brought up in a university town to which came Indian, African and Asiatic students in a variety of tints and hues. I was brought up to avoid them for reasons connected with local reputation and God's ordinances. You cannot easily go against what you were brought up to do unless you are a rebel by nature.

Anyhow, we visited George eventually, taking advantage of the offer of transport from some people bound north in search of game. He had heard of our arrival in Rhodesia and though he was glad, almost relieved, to see us he pursued a policy of sullenness for the first hour.

'We wanted to give you a surprise, George.'

'How were we to know that you'd get to hear of our arrival, George? News here must travel faster than light, George.'

'We did hope to give you a surprise, George.'

At last he said, 'Well, I must say it's good to see you. All we need now is Kathleen. We four simply must stick together. You find when you're in a place like this, there's nothing like old friends.'

He showed us his drying sheds. He showed us a paddock where he was experimenting with a horse and a zebra mare, attempting to mate them. They were frolicking happily, but not together. They passed each other in their private play time and again, but without acknowledgement and without resentment.

'It's been done before,' George said. 'It makes a fine strong beast, more intelligent than a mule and sturdier than a horse. But I'm not having any success with this pair, they won't look at each other.'

After a while, he said, 'Come in for a drink and meet Matilda.'

She was dark brown, with a subservient hollow chest and round shoulders, a gawky woman, very snappy with the house-boys. We said pleasant things as we drank on the stoep before dinner, but we found George difficult. For some reason he began to rail at me for breaking off my engagement to Skinny, saying what a dirty trick it was after all those good times in the old days. I diverted attention to Matilda. I supposed, I said, she knew this part of the country well?

'No,' said she, 'I been a-shellitered my life. I not put out to working. Me nothing to go from place to place is allowed like dirty girls does.' In her speech she gave every syllable equal stress.

George explained, 'Her father was a white magistrate in Natal. She had a sheltered upbringing, different from the other coloureds, you realize.'

'Man, me no black-eyed Susan,' said Matilda, 'no, no.'

On the whole, George treated her as a servant. She was about four months advanced in pregnancy, but he made her get up and fetch for him, many times. Soap: that was one of the things Matilda had to fetch. George made his own bath soap, showed it proudly, gave us the recipe which I did not trouble to remember; I was fond of nice soaps during my lifetime and George's smelt of brilliantine and looked likely to soil one's skin.

'D'yo brahn?' Matilda asked me.

George said, 'She is asking if you go brown in the sun.'

'No, I go freckled.'

'I got sister-in-law go freckles.'

She never spoke another word to Skinny nor to me, and we never saw her again.

Some months later I said to Skinny,

'I'm fed up with being a camp-follower.'

He was not surprised that I was leaving his unit, but he hated my way of expressing it. He gave me a Presbyterian look.

'Don't talk like that. Are you going back to England or staying?'

'Staying, for a while.'

'Well, don't wander too far off.'

I was able to live on the fee I got for writing a gossip column in a local weekly, which wasn't my idea of writing about life, of course. I made friends, more than I could cope with, after I left Skinny's exclusive little band of archaeologists. I had the attractions of being newly out from England and of wanting to see life. Of the countless young men and go-ahead families who purred me along the Rhodesian roads, hundred after hundred miles, I only kept up with one family when I returned to my native land. I think that was because they were the most representative, they stood for all the rest: people in those parts are very typical of each other, as one group of standing stones in that wilderness is like the next.

I met George once more in a hotel in Bulawayo. We drank highballs and spoke of war. Skinny's party were just then deciding whether to remain in the country or return home. They had reached an exciting part of their research, and whenever I got a chance to visit Zimbabwe he would take me for a moonlight walk in the ruined temple and try to make me see phantom Phoenicians flitting ahead of us, or along the walls. I had half a mind to marry Skinny; perhaps, I thought, when his studies were finished. The impending war was in our bones: so I remarked to George as we sat drinking highballs on the hotel stoep in the hard bright sunny July winter of that year.

George was inquisitive about my relations with Skinny. He tried to pump me for about half an hour and when at last I said, 'You are becoming aggressive, George,' he stopped. He became quite pathetic. He said, 'War or no war I'm clearing out of this.'

'It's the heat does it,' I said.

'I'm clearing out in any case. I've lost a fortune in tobacco. My uncle is making a fuss. It's the other bloody planters; once you get the wrong side of them you're finished in this wide land.'

'What about Matilda?' I asked.

He said, 'She'll be all right. She's got hundreds of relatives.'

I had already heard about the baby girl. Coal black, by repute, with George's features. And another on the way, they said.

'What about the child?'

He didn't say anything to that. He ordered more highballs and when they arrived he swizzled his for a long time with a stick. 'Why didn't you ask me to your twenty-first?' he said then.

'I didn't have anything special, no party, George. We had a quiet drink among ourselves, George, just Skinny and the old professors and two of the wives and me, George.'

'You didn't ask me to your twenty-first,' he said. 'Kathleen writes to me regularly.'

This wasn't true. Kathleen sent me letters fairly often in which she said, 'Don't tell George I wrote to you as he will be expecting word from me and I can't be bothered actually.'

'But you,' said George, 'don't seem to have any sense of old friendships, you and Skinny.'

'Oh, George!' I said.

'Remember the times we had,' George said. 'We used to have times.' His large brown eyes began to water.

'I'll have to be getting along,' I said.

'Please don't go. Don't leave me just yet. I've something to tell you.'

'Something nice?' I laid on an eager smile. All responses to George had to be overdone.

'You don't know how lucky you are,' George said.

'How?' I said. Sometimes I got tired of being called lucky by everybody. There were times when, privately practising my writings about life, I knew the bitter side of my fortune. When I failed again and again to reproduce life in some satisfactory and perfect form, I was the more imprisoned, for all my carefree living, within my craving for this satisfaction. Sometimes, in my impotence and need I secreted a venom which infected all my life for days on end and which spurted out indiscriminately on Skinny or on anyone who crossed my path.

'You aren't bound by anyone,' George said. 'You come and go as you please. Something always turns up for you. You're free, and you don't know your luck.'

'You're a damn sight more free than I am,' I said sharply. 'You've got your rich uncle.'

'He's losing interest in me,' George said. 'He's had enough.'

'Oh well, you're young yet. What was it you wanted to tell me?'

'A secret,' George said. 'Remember we used to have those secrets.'

'Oh, yes we did.'

'Did you ever tell any of mine?'

'Oh no, George.' In reality, I couldn't remember any particular secret out of the dozens we must have exchanged from our schooldays onwards.

'Well, this is a secret, mind. Promise not to tell.'

'Promise.'

'I'm married.'

'Married, George! Oh, who to?'

'Matilda.'

'How dreadful!' I spoke before I could think, but he agreed with me.

'Yes, it's awful, but what could I do?'

'You might have asked my advice,' I said pompously.

'I'm two years older than you are. I don't ask advice from you, Needle, little beast.'

'Don't ask for sympathy then.'

'A nice friend you are,' he said, 'I must say after all these years.'

'Poor George!' I said.

'There are three white men to one white woman in this country,' said George. 'An isolated planter doesn't see a white woman and if he sees one she doesn't see him. What could I do? I needed the woman.'

I was nearly sick. One, because of my Scottish upbringing. Two, because of my horror of corny phrases like 'I needed the woman', which George repeated twice again.

'And Matilda got tough,' said George, 'after you and Skinny came to visit us. She had some friends at the Mission, and she packed up and went to them.'

'You should have let her go,' I said.

'I went after her,' George said. 'She insisted on being married, so I married her.'

'That's not a proper secret, then,' I said. 'The news of a mixed marriage soon gets about.'

'I took care of that,' George said. 'Crazy as I was, I took her to the Congo and married her there. She promised to keep quiet about it.'

'Well, you can't clear off and leave her now, surely,' I said.

'I'm going to get out of this place. I can't stand the woman and I can't stand the country. I didn't realize what it would be like. Two years of the country and three months of my wife has been enough.'

'Will you get a divorce?'

'No. Matilda's Catholic. She won't divorce.'

George was fairly getting through the highballs, and I wasn't far behind him. His brown eyes floated shiny and liquid as he told me how he had written to tell his uncle of his plight. 'Except, of course, I didn't say we were married, that would have been too much for him. He's a prejudiced hardened old colonial. I only said I'd had a child by a coloured woman and was expecting another, and he perfectly understood. He came at once by plane a few weeks ago. He's made a settlement on her, providing she keeps her mouth shut about her association with me.'

'Will she do that?'

'Oh, yes, or she won't get the money.'

'But as your wife she has a claim on you, in any case.'

'If she claimed as my wife she'd get far less. Matilda knows what she's doing, greedy bitch she is. She'll keep her mouth shut.'

'Only, you won't be able to marry again, will you, George?'

'Not unless she dies,' he said. 'And she's as strong as a trek ox.'

'Well, I'm sorry, George,' I said.

'Good of you to say so,' he said. 'But I can see by your chin that you disapprove of me. Even my old uncle understood.'

'Oh, George, I quite understand. You were lonely, I suppose.'

'You didn't even ask me to your twenty-first. If you and Skinny had been nicer to me, I would never have lost my head and married the woman, never.'

'You didn't ask me to your wedding,' I said.

'You're a catty bissom, Needle, not like what you were in the old times when you used to tell us your wee stories.'

'I'll have to be getting along,' I said.

'Mind you keep the secret,' George said.

'Can't I tell Skinny? He would be very sorry for you, George.'

'You mustn't tell anyone. Keep it a secret. Promise.'

'Promise,' I said. I understood that he wished to enforce some sort of bond between us with this secret, and I thought. 'Oh well, I suppose he's lonely. Keeping his secret won't do any harm.'

I returned to England with Skinny's party just before the war.

I did not see George again till just before my death, five years ago.

After the war Skinny returned to his studies. He had two more exams, over a period of eighteen months, and I thought I might marry him when the exams were over.

'You might do worse than Skinny,' Kathleen used to say to me on our Saturday morning excursions to the antique shops and the junk stalls.

She too was getting on in years. The remainder of our families in Scotland were hinting that it was time we settled down with husbands. Kathleen was a little younger than me, but looked much older. She knew her chances were diminishing but at that time I did not think she cared very much. As for myself, the main attraction of marrying Skinny was his prospective expeditions to Mesopotamia. My desire to marry him had to be stimulated by the continual reading of books about Babylon and Assyria; perhaps Skinny felt this, because he supplied the books and even started instructing me in the art of deciphering cuneiform tables.

Kathleen was more interested in marriage than I thought. Like me, she had racketed around a good deal during the war; she had actually been engaged to an officer in the US navy, who was killed. Now she kept an antique shop near Lambeth, was doing very nicely, lived in a Chelsea square, but for all that she must have wanted to be married and have children. She would stop and look into all the prams which the mothers had left outside shops or area gates.

'The poet Swinburne used to do that,' I told her once.

'Really? Did he want children of his own?'

'I shouldn't think so. He simply liked babies.'

Before Skinny's final exam he fell ill and was sent to a sanatorium in Switzerland.

'You're fortunate after all not to be married to him,' Kathleen said. 'You might have caught TB.'

I was fortunate, I was lucky . . . so everyone kept telling me on different occasions. Although it annoyed me to hear, I knew they were right, but in a way that was different from what they meant. It took me very small effort to make a living; book reviews, odd jobs for Kathleen, a few months with the publicity man again, still getting up speeches about literature, art and life for industrial tycoons. I was waiting to write about life and it seemed to me that the good fortune lay in this, whenever it should be. And until then I was assured of my charmed life, the necessities of existence always coming my way and I with far more leisure than anyone else. I thought of my type of luck after I became a Catholic and was being confirmed. The Bishop touches the candidate on the cheek, a symbolic reminder of the sufferings a Christian is supposed to undertake. I thought, how lucky, what a feathery symbol to stand for the hellish violence of its true meaning.

I visited Skinny twice in the two years that he was in the sanatorium. He was almost cured, and expected to be home within a few months. I told Kathleen after my last visit.

'Maybe I'll marry Skinny when he's well again.'

'Make it definite, Needle, and not so much of the maybe. You don't know when you're well off,' she said.

This was five years ago, in the last year of my life. Kathleen and I had become very close friends. We met several times each week, and after our Saturday morning excursions in the Portobello Road very often I would accompany Kathleen to her aunt's house in Kent for a long week-end.

One day in the June of that year I met Kathleen specially for lunch because she had phoned me to say she had news.

'Guess who came into the shop this afternoon,' she said.

'Who?'

'George.'

We had half imagined George was dead. We had received no letters in the past ten years. Early in the war we had heard rumours of his keeping a night-club in Durban, but nothing after that. We could have made inquiries if we had felt moved to do so.

At one time, when we discussed him, Kathleen had said,

'I ought to get in touch with poor George. But then I think he would write back. He would demand a regular correspondence again.'

'We four must stick together,' I mimicked.

'I can visualize his reproachful limpid orbs,' Kathleen said.

Skinny said, 'He's probably gone native. With his coffee concubine and a dozen mahogany kids.'

'Perhaps he's dead,' Kathleen said.

I did not speak of George's marriage, nor of any of his confidences in the hotel at Bulawayo. As the years passed we ceased to mention him except in passing, as someone more or less dead so far as we were concerned.

Kathleen was excited about George's turning up. She had forgotten her impatience with him in former days; she said,

'It was so wonderful to see old George. He seems to need a friend, feels neglected, out of touch with things.'

'He needs mothering, I suppose.'

Kathleen didn't notice the malice. She declared, 'That's exactly the case with George. It always has been, I can see it now.'

She seemed ready to come to any rapid new and happy conclusion about George. In the course of the morning he had told her of his wartime night-club in Durban, his game-shooting expeditions since. It was clear he had not mentioned Matilda. He had put on weight, Kathleen told me, but he could carry it.

18

I was curious to see this version of George, but I was leaving for Scotland next day and did not see him till September of that year, just before my death.

While I was in Scotland I gathered from Kathleen's letters that she was seeing George very frequently, finding enjoyable company in him, looking after him. 'You'll be surprised to see how he has developed.' Apparently he would hang round Kathleen in her shop most days, 'it makes him feel useful' as she maternally expressed it. He had an old relative in Kent whom he visited at week-ends; this old lady lived a few miles from Kathleen's aunt, which made it easy for them to travel down together on Saturdays, and go for long country walks.

'You'll see such a difference in George,' Kathleen said on my return to London in September. I was to meet him that night, a Saturday. Kathleen's aunt was abroad, the maid on holiday, and I was to keep Kathleen company in the empty house.

George had left London for Kent a few days earlier. 'He's actually helping with the harvest down there!' Kathleen told me lovingly.

Kathleen and I planned to travel down together, but on that Saturday she was unexpectedly delayed in London on some business. It was arranged that I should go ahead of her in the early afternoon to see to the provisions for our party; Kathleen had invited George to dinner at her aunt's house that night.

'I should be with you by seven,' she said. 'Sure you won't mind the empty house? I hate arriving at empty houses, myself.'

I said no, I liked an empty house.

So I did, when I got there. I had never found the house more likeable. A large Georgian vicarage in about eight acres, most of the rooms shut and sheeted, there being only one servant. I discovered that I wouldn't need to go shopping, Kathleen's aunt had left many and delicate supplies with notes attached to them: 'Eat this up please do, see also fridge' and 'A treat for three hungry people see also 2 bttles beaune for yr party on back kn table.' It was like a treasure hunt as I followed clue after clue through the cool silent domestic quarters. A house in which there are no people – but with all the signs of tenancy – can be a most tranquil good place. People take up space in a house out of proportion to their size. On my previous visits I had seen the rooms overflowing, as it seemed, with Kathleen, her aunt, and the little fat maidservant; they were always on the move. As I wandered through that part of the house which was in use, opening windows to let in the pale yellow air of September, I was not conscious that I, Needle, was taking up any space at all, I might have been a ghost.

The only thing to be fetched was the milk. I waited till after four when the milking should be done, then set off for the farm which lay across two fields at the back of the orchard. There, when the byre-man was handing me the bottle, I saw George.

'Hallo, George,' I said.

'Needle! What are you doing here?' he said.

'Fetching milk,' I said.

'So am I. Well, it's good to see you, I must say.'

As we paid the farm-hand, George said, 'I'll walk back with you part of the way. But I mustn't stop, my old cousin's without any milk for her tea. How's Kathleen?'

'She was kept in London. She's coming on later, about seven, she expects.'

We had reached the end of the first field. George's way led to the left and on to the main road.

'We'll see you tonight, then?' I said.

'Yes, and talk about old times.'

'Grand,' I said.

But George got over the stile with me.

'Look here,' he said, 'I'd like to talk to you, Needle.'

'We'll talk tonight, George. Better not keep your cousin waiting for the milk.' I found myself speaking to him almost as if he were a child.

'No, I want to talk to you alone. This is a good opportunity.'

We began to cross the second field. I had been hoping to have the house to myself for a couple more hours and I was rather petulant.

'See,' he said suddenly, 'that haystack.'

'Yes,' I said absently.

'Let's sit there and talk. I'd like to see you up on a haystack again. I still keep that photo. Remember that time when –'

'I found the needle,' I said very quickly, to get it over.

But I was glad to rest. The stack had been broken up, but we managed to find a nest in it. I buried my bottle of milk in the hay for coolness. George placed his carefully at the foot of the stack.

'My old cousin is terribly vague, poor soul. A bit hazy in her head. She hasn't the least sense of time. If I tell her I've only been gone ten minutes she'll believe it.'

I giggled, and looked at him. His face had grown much larger, his lips full, wide, and with a ripe colour that is strange in a man. His brown eyes were abounding as before with some inarticulate plea.

'So you're going to marry Skinny after all these years?'

'I really don't know, George.'

'You played him up properly.'

'It isn't for you to judge. I have my own reasons for what I do.'

'Don't get sharp,' he said, 'I was only funning.' To prove it, he lifted a tuft of hay and brushed my face with it.

'D'you know,' he said next, 'I didn't think you and Skinny treated me very decently in Rhodesia.'

'Well, we were busy, George. And we were younger then, we had a lot to do and see. After all, we could see you any other time, George.'

'A touch of selfishness,' he said.

'I'll have to be getting along, George.' I made to get down from the stack.

He pulled me back. 'Wait, I've got something to tell you.'

'OK, George, tell me.'

'First promise not to tell Kathleen. She wants it kept a secret so that she can tell you herself.'

'All right. Promise.'

'I'm going to marry Kathleen.'

'But you're already married.'

Sometimes I heard news of Matilda from the one Rhodesian family with whom I still kept up. They referred to her as 'George's Dark Lady' and of course they did not know he was married to her. She had apparently made a good thing out of George, they said, for she minced around all tarted up, never did a stroke of work and was always unsettling the respectable coloured girls in their neighbourhood. According to accounts, she was a living example of the folly of behaving as George did.

'I married Matilda in the Congo,' George was saying.

'It would still be bigamy,' I said.

He was furious when I used that word bigamy. He lifted a

handful of hay as if he would throw it in my face, but controlling himself meanwhile he fanned it at me playfully.

'I'm not sure that the Congo marriage was valid,' he continued. 'Anyway, as far as I'm concerned, it isn't.'

'You can't do a thing like that,' I said.

'I need Kathleen. She's been decent to me. I think we were always meant for each other, me and Kathleen.'

'I'll have to be going,' I said.

But he put his knee over my ankles, so that I couldn't move. I sat still and gazed into space.

He tickled my face with a wisp of hay.

'Smile up, Needle,' he said; 'let's talk like old times.'

'Well?'

'No one knows about my marriage to Matilda except you and me.'

'And Matilda,' I said.

'She'll hold her tongue so long as she gets her payments. My uncle left an annuity for the purpose, his lawyers see to it.'

'Let me go, George.'

'You promised to keep it a secret,' he said, 'you promised.'

'Yes, I promised.'

'And now that you're going to marry Skinny, we'll be properly coupled off as we should have been years ago. We should have been – but youth! – our youth got in the way, didn't it?'

'Life got in the way,' I said.

'But everything's going to be all right now. You'll keep my secret, won't you? You promised.' He had released my feet. I edged a little farther from him.

I said, 'If Kathleen intends to marry you, I shall tell her that you're already married.'

'You wouldn't do a dirty trick like that, Needle? You're going   23 to be happy with Skinny, you wouldn't stand in the way of my –'

'I must, Kathleen's my best friend,' I said swiftly.

He looked as if he would murder me and he did, he stuffed hay into my mouth until it could hold no more, kneeling on my body to keep it still, holding both my wrists tight in his huge left hand. I saw the red full lines of his mouth and the white slit of his teeth last thing on earth. Not another soul passed by as he pressed my body into the stack, as he made a deep nest for me, tearing up the hay to make a groove the length of my corpse, and finally pulling the warm dry stuff in a mound over this concealment, so natural-looking in a broken haystack. Then George climbed down, took up his bottle of milk and went his way. I suppose that was why he looked so unwell when I stood, nearly five years later, by the barrow in the Portobello Road and said in easy tones, 'Hallo, George!'

The Haystack Murder was one of the notorious crimes of that year.

My friends said, 'A girl who had everything to live for.'

After a search that lasted twenty hours, when my body was found, the evening papers said, '"Needle" is found: in haystack!'

Kathleen, speaking from that Catholic point of view which takes some getting used to, said, 'She was at Confession only the day before she died – wasn't she lucky?'

The poor byre-hand who sold us the milk was grilled for hour after hour by the local police, and later by Scotland Yard. So was George. He admitted walking as far as the haystack with me, but he denied lingering there.

'You hadn't seen your friend for ten years?' the Inspector asked him.

'That's right,' said George.

'And you didn't stop to have a chat?'

'No. We'd arranged to meet later at dinner. My cousin was waiting for the milk, I couldn't stop.'

The old soul, his cousin, swore that he hadn't been gone more than ten minutes in all, and she believed it to the day of her death a few months later. There was the microscopic evidence of hay on George's jacket, of course, but the same evidence was on every man's jacket in the district that fine harvest year. Unfortunately, the byre-man's hands were even brawnier and mightier than George's. The marks on my wrists had been done by such hands, so the laboratory charts indicated when my post-mortem was all completed. But the wrist-marks weren't enough to pin down the crime to either man. If I hadn't been wearing my long-sleeved cardigan, it was said, the bruises might have matched up properly with someone's fingers.

Kathleen, to prove that George had absolutely no motive, told the police that she was engaged to him. George thought this a little foolish. They checked up on his life in Africa, right back to his living with Matilda. But the marriage didn't come out – who would think of looking up registers in the Congo? Not that this would have proved any motive for murder. All the same, George was relieved when the inquiries were over without the marriage to Matilda being disclosed. He was able to have his nervous breakdown at the same time as Kathleen had hers, and they recovered together and got married, long after the police had shifted their inquiries to an Air Force camp five miles from Kathleen's aunt's home. Only a lot of excitement and drinks came of those investigations. The Haystack Murder was one of the unsolved crimes that year.

Shortly afterwards the byre-hand emigrated to Canada to start afresh, with the help of Skinny who felt sorry for him.

After seeing George taken away home by Kathleen that Saturday in the Portobello Road, I thought that perhaps I might be seeing more of him in similar circumstances. The next Saturday I looked out for him, and at last there he was, without Kathleen, half-worried, half-hopeful.

I dashed his hopes. I said, 'Hallo, George!'

He looked in my direction, rooted in the midst of the flowing market-mongers in that convivial street. I thought to myself, 'He looks as if he had a mouthful of hay.' It was the new bristly maize-coloured beard and moustache surrounding his great mouth which suggested the thought, gay and lyrical as life.

'Hallo, George!' I said again.

I might have been inspired to say more on that agreeable morning, but he didn't wait. He was away down a side street and along another street and down one more, zig-zag, as far and as devious as he could take himself from the Portobello Road.

Nevertheless he was back again next week. Poor Kathleen had brought him in her car. She left it at the top of the street, and got out with him, holding him tight by the arm. It grieved me to see Kathleen ignoring the spread of scintillations on the stalls. I had myself seen a charming Battersea box quite to her taste, also a pair of enamelled silver earrings. But she took no notice of these wares, clinging close to George, and, poor Kathleen – I hate to say how she looked.

And George was haggard. His eyes seemed to have got smaller as if he had been recently in pain. He advanced up the road with Kathleen on his arm, letting himself lurch from side to side with his wife bobbing beside him, as the crowds asserted their rights of way.

'Oh, George!' I said. 'You don't look at all well, George.'

'Look!' said George. 'Over there by the hardware barrow. That's Needle.'

Kathleen was crying. 'Come back home, dear,' she said.

'Oh, you don't look well, George!' I said.

They took him to a nursing home. He was fairly quiet, except on Saturday mornings, when they had a hard time of it to keep him indoors and away from the Portobello Road.

But a couple of months later he did escape. It was a Monday.

They searched for him in the Portobello Road, but actually he had gone off to Kent to the village near the scene of the Haystack Murder. There he went to the police and gave himself up, but they could tell from the way he was talking that there was something wrong with the man.

'I saw Needle in the Portobello Road three Saturdays running,' he explained, 'and they put me in a private ward but I got away while the nurses were seeing to the new patient. You remember the murder of Needle – well, I did it. Now you know the truth, and that will keep bloody Needle's mouth shut.'

Dozens of poor mad fellows confess to every murder. The police obtained an ambulance to take him back to the nursing home. He wasn't there long. Kathleen gave up her shop and devoted herself to looking after him at home. But she found that the Saturday mornings were a strain. He insisted on going to see me in the Portobello Road and would come back to insist that he'd murdered Needle. Once he tried to tell her something about Matilda, but Kathleen was so kind and solicitous, I don't think he had the courage to remember what he had to say.

Skinny had always been rather reserved with George since the murder. But he was kind to Kathleen. It was he who persuaded them to emigrate to Canada so that George should be well out of reach of the Portobello Road.

George has recovered somewhat in Canada but of course he will never be the old George again, as Kathleen writes to Skinny. 'That Haystack tragedy did for George,' she writes. 'I feel sorrier for George sometimes than I am for poor Needle. But I do often have Masses said for Needle's soul.'

I doubt if George will ever see me again in the Portobello Road. He broods much over the crumpled snapshot he took of us on the haystack. Kathleen does not like the photograph, I don't wonder. For my part, I consider it quite a jolly snap, but I don't think we were any of us so lovely as we look in it, gazing blatantly over the ripe cornfields, Skinny with his humorous expression, I secure in my difference from the rest, Kathleen with her head prettily perched on her hand, each reflecting fearlessly in the face of George's camera the glory of the world, as if it would never pass.

Bang-bang You're Dead

At that time many of the men looked like Rupert Brooke, whose portrait still hung in everyone's imagination. It was that clear-cut, 'typically English' face which is seldom seen on the actual soil of England but proliferates in the African Colonies.

'I must say,' said Sybil's hostess, 'the men look charming.'

These men were all charming, Sybil had decided at the time, until you got to know them. She sat in the dark room watching the eighteen-year-old film unrolling on the screen as if the particular memory had solidified under the effect of some intense heat coming out of the projector. She told herself, I was young, I demanded nothing short of perfection. But then, she thought, that is not quite the case. But it comes to the same thing; to me, the men were not charming for long.

The first reel came to an end. Someone switched on the light. Her host picked the next film out of its tropical packing.

'It must be an interesting experience,' said her hostess, 'seeing yourself after all those years.'

'Hasn't Sybil seen these films before?' said a latecomer.

'No, never – have you, Sybil?'

'No, never.'

'If they had been my films,' said her hostess, 'my curiosity could not have waited eighteen years.'

The Kodachrome reels had lain in their boxes in the dark of Sybil's cabin trunk. Why bother, when one's memory was clear?

'Sybil didn't know anyone who had a projector,' said her hostess, 'until we got ours.'

'It was delightful,' said the latecomer, an elderly lady, 'what I saw of it. Are the others as good?'

Sybil thought for a moment. 'The photography is probably good,' she said. 'There was a cook behind the camera.'

'A cook! How priceless; whatever do you mean?' said her hostess.

'The cook-boy,' said Sybil, 'was trained up to use the camera.'

'He managed it well,' said her host, who was adjusting the new reel.

'Wonderful colours,' said her hostess. 'Oh, I'm so glad you dug them out. How healthy and tanned and open-necked everyone looks. And those adorable shiny natives all over the place.'

The elderly lady said, 'I liked the bit where you came out on the verandah in your shorts carrying the gun.'

'Ready?' said Sybil's host. The new reel was fixed. 'Put out the lights,' he said.

It was the stoep again. Through the french windows came a dark girl in shorts followed by a frisky young Alsatian.

'Lovely dog,' commented Sybil's host. 'He seems to be asking Sybil for a game.'

'That is someone else,' Sybil said very quickly.

'The girl there, with the dog?'

'Yes, of course. Don't you see me walking across the lawn by the trees?'

'Oh, of course, of course. She did look like you, Sybil, that girl with the dog. Wasn't she like Sybil? I mean, just as she came out on the verandah.'

'Yes, *I* thought it was Sybil for a moment until I saw Sybil in the background. But you can see the difference now. See, as she turns round. That girl isn't really like Sybil, it must be the shorts.'

'There was a slight resemblance between us,' Sybil remarked.

The projector purred on.

'Look, there's a little girl rather like you, Sybil.' Sybil, walking between her mother and father, one hand in each, had already craned round. The other child, likewise being walked along, had looked back too.

The other child wore a black velour hat turned up all round, a fawn coat of covert-coating, and at her neck a narrow white ermine tie. She wore white silk gloves. Sybil was dressed identically, and though this in itself was nothing to marvel at, since numerous small girls wore this ensemble when they were walked out in the parks and public gardens of cathedral towns in 1923, it did fortify the striking resemblance in features, build, and height, between the two children. Sybil suddenly felt she was walking past her own reflection in the long looking-glass. There was her peak chin, her black bobbed hair under her hat, with its fringe almost touching her eyebrows. Her wide-spaced eyes, her nose very small like a cat's. 'Stop staring, Sybil,' whispered her mother. Sybil had time to snatch the gleam of white socks and black patent leather button shoes. Her own socks were white but her shoes were brown, with laces. At first she felt this one discrepancy was wrong, in the sense that it was wrong to step on one of the cracks in the pavement. Then she felt it was right that there should be a difference.

'The Colemans,' Sybil's mother remarked to her father. 'They keep that hotel at Hillend. The child must be about Sybil's age. Very alike, aren't they? And I suppose,' she continued for Sybil's benefit, 'she's a good little girl like Sybil.' Quick-witted Sybil thought poorly of the last remark with its subtle counsel of perfection.

On other occasions, too, they passed the Coleman child on a Sunday walk. In summer time the children wore panama hats and tussore silk frocks discreetly adorned with drawn-thread work. Sometimes the Coleman child was accompanied by a young maid-servant in grey dress and black stockings. Sybil noted this one difference between her own entourage and the other girl's. 'Don't turn round and stare,' whispered her mother.

It was not till she went to school that she found Désirée Coleman to be a year older than herself. Désirée was in a higher class but sometimes, when the whole school was assembled on the lawn or in the gym, Sybil would be, for a few moments, mistaken for Désirée. In the late warm spring the classes sat in separate groups under the plane trees until, as by simultaneous instinct, the teachers would indicate time for break. The groups would mingle, and 'Sybil, dear, your shoe-lace,' a teacher might call out; and then, as Sybil regarded her neat-laced shoes, 'Oh no, not Sybil, I mean Désirée.' In the percussion band Sybil banged her triangle triumphantly when the teacher declared, '*Much* better than yesterday, Sybil.' But she added, 'I mean Désirée.'

Only the grown-ups mistook one child for another at odd moments. None of her small companions made this mistake. After the school concert Sybil's mother said, 'For a second I thought you were Désirée in the choir. It's strange you are so alike. I'm not a bit like Mrs Coleman and your daddy doesn't resemble *him* in the least.'

Sybil found Désirée unsatisfactory as a playmate. Sybil was precocious, her brain was like a blade. She had discovered that dull children were apt to be spiteful. Désirée would sit innocently cross-legged beside you at a party, watching the conjurer, then suddenly, for no apparent reason, jab at you viciously with her elbow.

By the time Sybil was eight and Désirée nine it was seldom that anyone, even strangers and new teachers, mixed them up. Sybil's nose became more sharp and pronounced while Désirée's seemed to sink into her plump cheeks like a painted-on nose. Only on a few occasions, and only on dark winter afternoons between the last of three o'clock daylight and the coming on of lights all over the school, was Sybil mistaken for Désirée.

Between Sybil's ninth year and her tenth Désirée's family came to live in her square. The residents' children were taken to the gardens of the square after school by mothers and nurse-maids, and were bidden to play with each other nicely. Sybil regarded the intrusion of Désirée sulkily, and said she preferred her book. She cheered up, however, when a few weeks later the Dobell boys came to live in the square. The two Dobells had dusky-rose skins and fine dark eyes. It appeared the father was half Indian.

How Sybil adored the Dobells! They were a new type of playmate in her experience, so jumping and agile, and yet so gentle, so unusually courteous. Their dark skins were never dirty, a fact which Sybil obscurely approved. She did not then mind Désirée joining in their games; the Dobell boys were a kind of charm against despair, for they did not understand stupidity and so did not notice Désirée's.

The girl lacked mental stamina, could not keep up an imagina-tive game for long, was shrill and apt to kick her playmates unaccountably and on the sly; the Dobells reacted to this with a simple resignation. Perhaps the lack of opposition was the reason that Désirée continually shot Sybil dead, contrary to the rules, whenever she felt like it.

Sybil resented with the utmost passion the repeated daily massacre of herself before the time was ripe. It was useless for Jon Dobell to explain, 'Not yet, Désirée. Wait, wait, Désirée. She's not to be shot down yet. She hasn't crossed the bridge yet, and you can't shoot her from there, anyway – there's a big boulder between you and her. You have to creep round it, and Hugh has a shot at you first, and he thinks he's got you, but only your hat. And . . .'

It was no use. Each day before the game started the four sat in conference on the short dry prickly grass. The proceedings were agreed. The game was on. 'Got it all clear, Désirée?' 'Yes,' she said, every day. Désirée shouted and got herself excited, she made foolish sounds even when supposed to be stalking the bandits through the silent forest. A few high screams and then, 'Bang-bang,' she yelled, aiming at Sybil, 'you're dead.' Sybil obediently rolled over, protesting none the less that the game had only begun, while the Dobells sighed, 'Oh, *Désirée*!'

Sybil vowed to herself each night, I will do the same to her. Next time – tomorrow if it isn't raining – I will bang-bang her before she has a chance to hang her panama on the bough as a decoy. I will say bang-bang on her out of turn, and I will do her dead before her time.

But on no succeeding tomorrow did Sybil bring herself to do this. Her pride before the Dobells was more valuable than the success of the game. Instead, with her cleverness, Sybil set herself to avoid Désirée's range for as long as possible. She dodged behind the laurels and threw out a running commentary as if to a mental defective, such as, 'I'm in disguise, all in green, and no one can see me among the trees.' But still Désirée saw her. Désirée's eyes insisted on penetrating solid mountains. 'I'm half a mile away from everyone,' Sybil cried as Désirée's gun swivelled relentlessly upon her.

I shall refuse to be dead, Sybil promised herself. I'll break the rule. If it doesn't count with her why should it count with me? I won't roll over any more when she bangs you're dead to me. Next time, tomorrow if it isn't raining . . .

But Sybil simply did roll over. When Jon and Hugh Dobell called out to her that Désirée's bang-bang did not count she started hopefully to resurrect herself; but 'It does count, it *does*. That's the rule,' Désirée counter-screeched. And Sybil dropped back flat, knowing utterly that this was final.

And so the girl continued to deal premature death to Sybil, losing her head, but never so much that she aimed at one of the boys. For some reason which Sybil did not consider until she was years and years older, it was always herself who had to die.

One day, when Désirée was late in arriving for play, Sybil put it to the boys that Désirée should be left out of the game in future. 'She only spoils it.'

'But,' said Jon, 'you need four people for the game.'

'You need four,' said Hugh.

'No, you can do it with three.' As she spoke she was inventing the game with three. She explained to them what was in her mind's eye. But neither boy could grasp the idea, having got used to Bandits and Riders with two on each side. 'I am the lone Rider, you see,' said Sybil. 'Or,' she wheedled, 'the cherry tree can be a Rider.' She was talking to stone, inoffensive but uncomprehending. All at once she realized, without articulating the idea, that her intelligence was superior to theirs, and she felt lonely.

'Could we play rounders instead?' ventured Jon.

Sybil brought a book every day after that, and sat reading

beside her mother, who was glad, on the whole, that Sybil had grown tired of rowdy games.

'They were preparing,' said Sybil, 'to go on a shoot.'

Sybil's host was changing the reel.

'I get quite a new vision of Sybil,' said her hostess, 'seeing her in such a . . . such a *social* environment. Were any of these people intellectuals, Sybil?'

'No, but lots of poets.'

'Oh, *no*. Did they all write poetry?'

'Quite a lot of them,' said Sybil, 'did.'

'Who *were* they all? Who was that blond fellow who was standing by the van with you?'

'He was the manager of the estate. They grew passion-fruit and manufactured the juice.'

'Passion-fruit – how killing. Did *he* write poetry?'

'Oh, yes.'

'And who was the girl, the one I thought was you?'

'Oh, I had known her as a child and we met again in the Colony. The short man was her husband.'

'And were you all off on safari that morning? I simply can't imagine you shooting anything, Sybil, somehow.'

'On this occasion,' said Sybil, 'I didn't go. I just held the gun for effect.'

Everyone laughed.

'Do you still keep up with these people? I've heard that colonials are great letter-writers, it keeps them in touch with –'

'No.' And she added, 'Three of them are dead. The girl and her husband, and the fair fellow.'

'Really? What happened to them? Don't tell me *they* were
mixed up in shooting affairs.'

'They were mixed up in shooting affairs,' said Sybil.

'Oh, these colonials,' said the elderly woman, 'and their shooting affairs!'

'Number three,' said Sybil's host. 'Ready? Lights out, please.'

'Don't get eaten by lions. I say, Sybil, don't get mixed up in a shooting affair.' The party at the railway station were unaware of the noise they were making for they were inside the noise. As the time of departure drew near Donald's relatives tended to herd themselves apart while Sybil's clustered round the couple.

'Two years – it will be an interesting experience for them.'

'Mind out for the shooting affairs. Don't let Donald have a gun.'

There had been an outbreak of popular headlines about the shooting affairs in the Colony. Much had been blared forth about the effect, on the minds of young settlers, of the climate, the hard drinking, the shortage of white women. The Colony was a place where lovers shot husbands, or shot themselves, where husbands shot natives who spied through bedroom windows. Letters to *The Times* arrived belatedly from respectable colonists, refuting the scandals with sober statistics. The recent incidents, they said, did not represent the habits of the peaceable majority. The Governor told the press that everything had been highly exaggerated. By the time Sybil and Donald left for the Colony the music-hall comics had already exhausted the entertainment value of colonial shooting affairs.

'Don't make pets of snakes or crocs. Mind out for the lions. Don't forget to write.'

It was almost a surprise to them to find that shooting affairs in the Colony were not entirely a music-hall myth. They occurred in waves. For three months at a time the gun-murders and

37

suicides were reported weekly. The old colonists with their very blue eyes sat beside their whisky bottles and remarked that another young rotter had shot himself. Then the rains would break and the shootings would cease for a long season.

Eighteen months after their marriage Donald was mauled by a lioness and died on the long stretcher journey back to the station. He was one of a party of eight. No one could really say how it happened; it was done in a flash. The natives had lost their wits, and, instead of shooting the beast, had come calling 'Ah-ah-ah,' and pointing to the spot. A few strides, shouldering the grass aside, and Donald's friends got the lioness as she reared from his body.

His friends in the archaeological team to which he belonged urged Sybil to remain in the Colony for the remaining six months, and return to England with them. Still undecided, she went on a sight-seeing tour. But before their time was up the archaeologists had been recalled. War had been declared. Civilians were not permitted to leave the continent, and Sybil was caught, like Donald under the lioness.

She wished he had lived to enjoy a life of his own, as she intended to do. It was plain to her that they must have separated had he lived. There had been no disagreement but, thought Sybil, given another two years there would have been disagreements. Donald had shown signs of becoming a bore. By the last, the twenty-seventh, year of his life, his mind had ceased to inquire. Archaeology, that thrilling subject, had become Donald's job, merely. He began to talk as if all archaeological methods and theories had ceased to evolve on the day he obtained his degree; it was now only a matter of applying his knowledge to field-work for a limited period. Archaeological papers came out from England. The usual crank literature on roneo foolscap followed them from one postal address to another. 'Donald, aren't you going to look through them?' Sybil said, as the journals and papers piled up. 'No, really, I don't see it's necessary.' It was not necessary because his future was fixed; two years in the field and then a lectureship. If it were my subject, she thought, these papers would be necessary to me. Even the crackpot ones, rightly read, would be, to me, enlarging.

Sybil lay in bed in the mornings reading the translation of Kierkegaard's *Journals*, newly arrived from England in their first, revelatory month of publication. She felt like a desert which had not realized its own aridity till the rain began to fall upon it. When Donald came home in the late afternoons she had less and less to say to him.

'There has been another shooting affair,' Donald said, 'across the valley. The chap came home unexpectedly and found his wife with another man. He shot them both.'

'In this place, one is never far from the jungle,' Sybil said.

'What are you talking about? We are eight hundred miles from the jungle.'

When he had gone on his first big shoot, eight hundred miles away in the jungle, she had reflected, there is no sign of a living mind in him, it is like a landed fish which has ceased to palpitate. But, she thought, another woman would never notice it. Other women do not wish to be married to a Mind. Yet I do, she thought, and I am a freak and should not have married. In fact I am not the marrying type. Perhaps that is why he does not explore my personality, any more than he reads the journals. It might make him think, and that would be hurtful.

After his death she wished he had lived to enjoy a life of his own, whatever that might have been. She took a job in a private school for girls and cultivated a few friends for diversion until the war should be over. Charming friends need not possess minds.

Their motor launch was rocking up the Zambesi. Sybil was leaning over the rail mouthing something to a startled native in a canoe. Now Sybil was pointing across the river.

'I think I was asking him,' Sybil commented to her friends in the darkness, 'about the hippo. There was a school of hippo some distance away, and we wanted to see them better. But the native said we shouldn't go too near – that's why he's looking so frightened – because the hippo often upset a boat, and then the crocs quickly slither into the water. There, look! We got a long shot of the hippo – those bumps in the water, like submarines, those are the snouts of hippo.'

The film rocked with the boat as it proceeded up the river. The screen went white.

'Something's happened,' said Sybil's hostess.

'Put on the light,' said Sybil's host. He fiddled with the projector and a young man, their lodger from upstairs, went to help him.

'I loved those tiny monkeys on the island,' said her hostess. 'Do hurry, Ted. What's gone wrong?'

'Shut up a minute,' he said.

'Sybil, you know you haven't changed much since you were a girl.'

'Thank you, Ella.' I haven't changed at all so far as I still think charming friends need not possess minds.

'I expect this will revive your memories, Sybil. The details, I mean. One is bound to forget so much.'

'Oh yes,' Sybil said, and she added, 'but I recall quite a lot of details, you know.'

'Do you *really*, Sybil?'

I wish, she thought, they wouldn't cling to my least word.

The young man turned from the projector with several feet of the film-strip looped between his widespread hands. 'Is the fair chap your husband, Mrs Greeves?' he said to Sybil.

'Sybil lost her husband very early on,' her hostess informed him in a low and sacred voice.

'Oh, I *am* sorry.'

Sybil's hostess replenished the drinks of her three guests. Her host turned from the projector, finished his drink, and passed his glass to be refilled, all in one movement. Everything they do seems large and important, thought Sybil. But I must not let it be so. We are only looking at old films.

She overheard a sibilant 'Whish-sh-sh?' from the elderly woman in which she discerned, 'Who is she?'

'Sybil Greeves,' her hostess breathed back, 'a distant cousin of Ted's through marriage.'

'Oh yes?' The low tones were puzzled as if all had not been explained.

'She's quite famous, of course.'

'Oh, I didn't know that.'

'Very few people know it,' said Sybil's hostess with a little arrogance.

'OK,' said Ted, 'lights out.'

'I must say,' said his wife, 'the colours are marvellous.'

All the time she was in the Colony Sybil longed for the inexplicable colourings of her native land. The flamboyants were too rowdy, the birds, the native women with their heads bound in cloth of piercing pink, their blinding black skin and white teeth, the baskets full of bright tough flowers or oranges on their 41 heads, the sight of which everyone else admired ('How I wish I could paint all this!') distressed Sybil, it bored her.

She rented a house, sharing it with a girl whose husband was fighting in the north. She was twenty-two. To safeguard her privacy absolutely, she had a plywood partition put up in the sitting-room, for it was another ten years before she had learnt those arts of leading a double life and listening to people ambiguously, which enabled her to mix without losing identity, and to listen without boredom.

On the other side of the partition Ariadne Lewis decorously entertained her friends, most of whom were men on leave. On a few occasions Sybil attended these parties, working herself, as in a frenzy of self-discipline, into a state of carnal excitement over the men. She managed to do this only by an effortful sealing-off of all her critical faculties except those which assessed a good male voice and appearance. The hangovers were frightful.

The scarcity of white girls made it easy for any one of them to keep a number of men in perpetual attendance. Ariadne had many boy-friends but no love affairs. Sybil had three affairs in the space of two years, to put herself to the test. They started at private dances, in the magnolia-filled gardens that smelt like a scent factory, under the Milky Way which looked like an over-crowded jeweller's window. The affairs ended when she suc-cumbed to one of her attacks of tropical flu, and lay in a twilight of the senses on a bed which had been set on the stone stoep and overhung with a white mosquito net like something bridal. With damp shaky hands she would write a final letter to the man and give it to her half-caste maid to post. He would telephone next morning, and would be put off by the house-boy, who was quite intelligent.

42   For some years she had been thinking she was not much

inclined towards sex. After the third affair, this dawned and rose within her as a whole realization, as if in the past, when she had told herself, 'I am not predominantly a sexual being,' or 'I'm rather a frigid freak, I suppose,' these were the sayings of an illiterate, never quite rational and known until now, but after the third affair the notion was so intensely conceived as to be almost new. It appalled her. She lay on the shady stoep, her fever subsiding, and examined her relations with men. She thought, what if I married again? She shivered under the hot sheet. Can it be, she thought, that I have a suppressed tendency towards women? She lay still and let the idea probe round in imagination. She surveyed, with a stony inward eye, all the women she had known, prim little academicians with cream peter-pan collars on their dresses, large dominant women, a number of beauties, conventional nitwits like Ariadne. No, really, she thought; neither men nor women. It is a not caring for sexual relations. It is not merely a lack of pleasure in sex, it is dislike of the excitement. And it is not merely dislike, it is worse, it is boredom.

She felt a lonely emotion near to guilt. The three love affairs took on heroic aspects in her mind. They were an attempt, thought Sybil, to do the normal thing. Perhaps I may try again. Perhaps, if I should meet the right man . . . But at the idea 'right man' she felt a sense of intolerable desolation and could not stop shivering. She raised the mosquito net and reached for the lemon juice, splashing it jerkily into the glass. She sipped. The juice had grown warm and had been made too sweet, but she let it linger on her sore throat and peered through the net at the backs of houses and the yellow veldt beyond them.

Ariadne said one morning, 'I met a girl last night, it was funny, I thought it was you at first and called over to her. But she wasn't really like you close up, it was just an impression. As a matter of fact, she knows you. I've asked her to tea, I forget her name.'

'I don't,' said Sybil.

But when Désirée arrived they greeted each other with exaggerated warmth, wholly felt at the time, as acquaintances do when they meet in another hemisphere. Sybil had last seen Désirée at a dance in Hampstead, and there had merely said, 'Oh, hallo.'

'We were at our first school together,' Désirée explained to Ariadne, still holding Sybil's hand.

Already Sybil wished to withdraw. 'It's strange,' she remarked, 'how, sooner or later, everyone in the Colony meets someone they have known, or their parents knew, at home.'

Désirée and her husband, Barry Weston, were settled in a remote part of the Colony. Sybil had heard of Weston, unaware that Désirée was his wife. He was much talked of as an enterprising planter. Some years ago he had got the idea of manufacturing passion-fruit juice, had planted orchards and set up a factory. The business was now expanding wonderfully. Barry Weston also wrote poetry, a volume of which, entitled *Home Thoughts*, he had published and sold with great success within the confines of the Colony. His first wife had died of blackwater fever. On one of his visits to England he had met and married Désirée, who was twelve years his junior.

'You *must* come and see us,' said Désirée to Sybil; and to Ariadne she explained again, 'We were at our first little private school together.' And she said 'Oh, Sybil, do you remember Trotsky? Do you remember Minnie Mouse, what a hell of a life we gave her? I shall never forget that day when . . .'

The school where Sybil taught was shortly to break up for holidays; Ariadne was to visit her husband in Cairo at that time.

Sybil promised a visit to the Westons. When Désirée, beautifully dressed in linen suiting, had departed, Ariadne said, 'I'm so glad you're going to stay with them. I hated the thought of your being all alone for the next few weeks.'

'Do you know,' Sybil said, 'I don't think I shall go to stay with them after all. I'll make an excuse.'

'Oh, why not? Oh, Sybil, it's such a lovely place, and it will be fun for you. He's a poet, too.' Sybil could sense exasperation, could hear Ariadne telling her friends, 'There's something wrong with Sybil. You never know a person till you live with them. Now Sybil will say one thing one minute, and the next ... Something wrong with her sex-life, perhaps ... odd ...'

At home, thought Sybil, it would not be such a slur. Her final appeal for a permit to travel to England had just been dismissed. The environment mauled her weakness. 'I think I'm going to have a cold,' she said, shivering.

'Go straight to bed, dear.' Ariadne called for black Elijah and bade him prepare some lemon juice. But the cold did not materialize.

She returned with flu, however, from her first visit to the Westons. Her 1936 Ford V8 had broken down on the road and she had waited three chilly hours before another car had appeared.

'You must get a decent car,' said the chemist's wife, who came to console her. 'These old crocks simply won't stand up to the roads out here.'

Sybil shivered and held her peace. Nevertheless, she returned to the Westons at mid-term.

Désirée's invitations were pressing, almost desperate. Again and again Sybil went in obedience to them. The Westons were a magnetic field.

There was a routine attached to her arrival. The elegant wicker chair was always set for her in the same position on the stoep. The same cushions, it seemed, were always piled in exactly the same way.

'What will you drink, Sybil? Are you comfy there, Sybil? We're going to give you a wonderful time, Sybil.' She was their little orphan, she supposed. She sat, with very dark glasses, contemplating the couple. 'We've planned – haven't we, Barry? – a surprise for you, Sybil.' 'We've planned – haven't we, Désirée? – a marvellous trip . . . a croc hunt . . . hippo . . .'

Sybil sips her gin and lime. Facing her on the wicker sofa, Désirée and her husband sit side by side. They gaze at Sybil affectionately. 'Take off your smoked glasses, Sybil, the sun's nearly gone,' Sybil takes them off. The couple hold hands. They peck kisses at each other, and presently, outrageously, they are entwined in a long erotic embrace in the course of which Barry once or twice regards Sybil from the corner of his eye. Barry disengages himself and sits with his arm about his wife; she snuggles up to him. Why, thinks Sybil, is this performance being staged? 'Sybil is shocked,' Barry remarks. She sips her drink, and reflects that a public display between man and wife somehow is more shocking than are courting couples in parks and doorways. 'We're very much in love with each other,' Barry explains, squeezing his wife. And Sybil wonders what is wrong with their marriage since obviously something is wrong. The couple kiss again. Am I dreaming this? Sybil asks herself.

Even on her first visit Sybil knew definitely there was something wrong with the marriage. She thought of herself, at first, as an objective observer, and was even amused when she understood they had chosen her to be their sort of Victim of Expiation. On occasions when other guests were present she noted that the love scenes did not take place. Instead, the couple tended to snub Sybil before their friends. 'Poor little Sybil, she lives all alone and is a teacher, and hasn't many friends. We have her here to stay as often as possible.' The people would look uneasily at Sybil, and would smile. 'But you must have *heaps* of friends,' they would say politely. Sybil came to realize she was an object of the Westons' resentment, and that, nevertheless, they found her indispensable.

Ariadne returned from Cairo. 'You always look washed out when you've been staying at the Westons',' she told Sybil eventually. 'I suppose it's due to the late parties and lots of drinks.'

'I suppose so.'

Désirée wrote continually. 'Do come, Barry needs you. He needs your advice about some sonnets.' Sybil tore up these letters quickly, but usually went. Not because her discomfort was necessary to their wellbeing, but because it was somehow necessary to her own. The act of visiting the Westons alleviated her sense of guilt.

I believe, she thought, they must discern my abnormality. How could they have guessed? She was always cautious when they dropped questions about her private life. But one's closest secrets have a subtle way of communicating themselves to the resentful vigilance of opposite types. I do believe, she thought, that heart speaks unto heart, and deep calleth unto deep. But rarely in clear language. There is a misunderstanding here. They imagine their demonstrations of erotic bliss will torment my frigid soul, and so far they are right. But the reason for my pain is not envy. Really, it is boredom.

Her Ford V8 rattled across country. How bored, she thought, I am going to be by their married tableau! How pleased, exultant, they will be! These thoughts consoled her, they were an offering to the gods.

'Are you comfy, Sybil?'

She sipped her gin and lime. 'Yes, thanks.'

His pet name for Désirée was Dearie. 'Kiss me, Dearie,' he said.

'There, Baddy,' his wife said to Barry, snuggling close to him and squinting at Sybil.

'I say, Sybil,' Barry said as he smoothed down his hair, 'you ought to get married again. You're missing such a lot.'

'Yes, Sybil,' said Désirée, 'you should either marry or enter a convent, one or the other.'

'I don't see why,' Sybil said, 'I should fit into a tidy category.'

'Well, you're neither one thing nor another – is she, honeybunch?'

True enough, thought Sybil, and that is why I'm laid out on the altar of boredom.

'Or get yourself a boy-friend,' said Désirée. 'It would be good for you.'

'You're wasting your best years,' said Barry.

'Are you comfy there, Sybil? ... We want you to enjoy yourself here. Any time you want to bring a boy-friend, we're broadminded – aren't we, Baddy?'

'Kiss me, Dearie,' he said.

Désirée took his handkerchief from his pocket and rubbed lipstick from his mouth. He jerked his head away and said to Sybil, 'Pass your glass.'

Désirée looked at her reflection in the glass of the french windows and said, 'Sybil's too intellectual, that's her trouble.'

She patted her hair, then looked at Sybil with an old childish enmity.

After dinner Barry would read his poems. Usually, he said, 'I'm not going to be an egotist tonight. I'm not going to read my poems.' And usually Désirée would cry, 'Oh do, Barry, do.' Always, eventually, he did. 'Marvellous,' Désirée would comment, 'wonderful.' By the third night of her visits, the farcical aspect of it all would lose its fascination for Sybil, and boredom would fill her near to bursting point, like gas in a balloon. To relieve the strain, she would sigh deeply from time to time. Barry was too engrossed in his own voice to notice this, but Désirée was watching. At first Sybil worded her comments tactfully. 'I think you should devote more of your time to your verses,' she said. And, since he looked puzzled, added, 'You owe it to poetry if you write it.'

'Nonsense,' said Désirée, 'he often writes a marvellous sonnet before shaving in the morning.'

'Sybil may be right,' said Barry. 'I owe poetry all the time I can give.'

'Are you tired, Sybil?' said Désirée. 'Why are you sighing like that; are you all right?'

Later, Sybil gave up the struggle and wearily said, 'Very good,' or 'Nice rhythm,' after each poem. And even the guilt of condoning Désirée's 'marvellous . . . wonderful' was less than the guilt of her isolated mind. She did not know then that the price of allowing false opinions was the gradual loss of one's capacity for forming true ones.

Not every morning, but at least twice during each visit Sybil would wake to hear the row in progress. The nanny, who brought her early tea, made large eyes and tiptoed warily. Sybil would have her bath, splashing a lot to drown the noise of the quarrel. Downstairs, the battle of voices descended, filled every room and corridor. When, on the worst occasions, the sound of shattering glass broke through the storm, Sybil would know that Barry was smashing up Désirée's dressing-table; and would wonder how Désirée always managed to replace her crystal bowls, since goods of that type were now scarce, and why she bothered to do so. Sybil would always find the two girls of Barry's former marriage standing side by side on the lawn frankly gazing up at the violent bedroom window. The nanny would cart off Désirée's baby for a far-away walk. Sybil would likewise disappear for the morning.

The first time this happened, Désirée told her later, 'I'm afraid you unsettle Barry.'

'What do you mean?' said Sybil.

Désirée dabbed her watery eyes and blew her nose. 'Well, of *course*, it stands to reason, Sybil, you're out to attract Barry. And he's only a man. I know you do it *unconsciously*, but . . .'

'I can't stand this sort of thing. I shall leave right away,' Sybil said.

'No, Sybil, no. Don't make a *thing* of it. Barry needs you. You're the only person in the Colony who can really talk to him about his poetry.'

'Understand,' said Sybil on that first occasion, 'I am not at all interested in your husband. I think he's an all-round third-rater. That is my opinion.'

Désirée looked savage. 'Barry,' she shouted, 'has made a fortune out of passion-fruit juice in eight years. He has sold four thousand copies of *Home Thoughts* on his own initiative.'

It was like a game for three players. According to the rules, she was to be in love, unconsciously, with Barry, and tortured by the contemplation of Désirée's married bliss. She felt too old to join in, just at that moment.

50

Barry came to her room while she was packing. 'Don't go,' he said. 'We need you. And after all, we are only human. What's a row? These quarrels only happen in the best marriages. And I can't for the life of me think how it started.'

'What a beautiful house. What a magnificent estate,' said Sybil's hostess.

'Yes,' said Sybil, 'it was the grandest in the Colony.'

'Were the owners frightfully grand?'

'Well, they were rich, of course.'

'I can see that. What a beautiful interior. I adore those lovely old oil lamps. I suppose you didn't have electricity?'

'Yes, there was electric light in all the rooms. But my friends preferred the oil-lamp tradition for the dining-room. You see, it was a copy of an old Dutch house.'

'Absolutely charming.'

The reel came to an end. The lights went up and everyone shifted in their chairs.

'What were those large red flowers?' said the elderly lady.

'Flamboyants.'

'Magnificent,' said her hostess. 'Don't you miss the colours, Sybil?'

'No, I don't, actually. There was too much of it for me.'

'You didn't care for the bright colours?' said the young man, leaning forward eagerly.

Sybil smiled at him.

'I liked the bit where those little lizards were playing among the stones. That was an excellent shot,' said her host. He was adjusting the last spool.

'I rather liked that handsome blond fellow,' said her hostess, as if the point had been in debate. 'Was he the passion-fruiter?' 51

'He was the manager,' said Sybil.

'Oh yes, you told me. He was in a shooting affair, did you say?'

'Yes, it was unfortunate.'

'Poor young man. It sounds quite a dangerous place. I suppose the sun and everything . . .'

'It was dangerous for some people. It depended.'

'The blacks look happy enough. Did you have any trouble with them in those days?'

'No,' said Sybil, 'only with the whites.'

Everyone laughed.

'Right,' said her host. 'Lights out, please.'

Sybil soon perceived the real cause of the Westons' quarrels. It differed from their explanations: they were both, they said, so much in love, so jealous of each other's relations with the opposite sex.

'Barry was furious,' said Désirée one day, '– weren't you, Barry? – because I smiled, merely smiled, at Carter.'

'I'll have it out with Carter,' muttered Barry. 'He's always hanging round Désirée.'

David Carter was their manager. Sybil was so foolish as once to say, 'Oh, surely David wouldn't –'

'Oh, wouldn't he?' said Désirée.

'Oh, wouldn't he?' said Barry.

Possibly they did not themselves know the real cause of their quarrels. These occurred on mornings when Barry had decided to lounge in bed and write poetry. Désirée, anxious that the passion-fruit business should continue to expand, longed for him to be at his office in the factory at eight o'clock each morning, by which time all other enterprising men in the Colony were at work. But Barry spoke more and more of retiring and devoting his time to his poems. When he lay abed, pen in hand, worrying a sonnet, Désirée would sulk and bang doors. The household knew that the row was on. 'Quiet! Don't you see I'm trying to think,' he would shout. '*I* suggest,' she would reply, 'you go to the library if you want to write.' It was evident that her greed and his vanity, facing each other in growling antipathy, were too terrible for either to face. Instead, the names of David Carter and Sybil would fly between them, consoling them, pepping-up and propagating the myth of their mutual attraction.

'Rolling your eyes at Carter in the orchard. Don't think I didn't notice.'

'Carter? That's funny. I can easily keep Carter in his place. But while we're on the subject, what about you with Sybil? You sat up late enough with her last night after I'd gone to bed.'

Sometimes he not only smashed the crystal bowls, he hurled them through the window.

In the exhausted afternoon Barry would explain. 'Désirée was upset – weren't you, Désirée – because of you, Sybil. It's understandable. We shouldn't stay up late talking after Désirée has gone to bed. You're a little devil in your way, Sybil.'

'Oh, well,' said Sybil obligingly, 'that's how it is.'

She became tired of the game. When, in the evenings, Barry's voice boomed forth with sonorous significance as befits a hallowed subject, she no longer thought of herself as an objective observer. She had tired of the game because she was now more than nominally committed to it. She ceased to be bored by the Westons; she began to hate them.

'What I don't understand,' said Barry, 'is why my poems are ignored back in England. I've sold over four thousand of the book out here. Feature articles about me have appeared in all the papers out here; remind me to show you them. But I can't get a single notice in London. When I send a poem to any of the magazines I don't even get a reply.'

'They are engaged in a war,' Sybil said.

'But they still publish poetry. Poetry so-called. Utter rubbish, all of it. You can't understand the stuff.'

'Yours is too good for them,' said Sybil. To a delicate ear her tone might have resembled the stab of a pin stuck into a waxen image.

'That's a fact, between ourselves,' said Barry. 'I shouldn't say it, but that's the answer.'

Barry was over-weight, square and dark. His face had lines, as of anxiety or stomach trouble. David Carter, when he passed, cool and fair through the house, was quite a change.

'England is finished,' said Barry. 'It's degenerate.'

'I wonder,' said Sybil, 'you have the heart to go on writing so cheerily about the English towns and countryside.' Now, now, Sybil, she thought; business is business, and the nostalgic English scene is what the colonists want. This visit must be my last. I shall not come again.

'Ah, that,' Barry was saying, 'was the England I remember. The good old country. But now, I'm afraid, it's decadent. After the war it will be no more than . . .'

Désirée would have the servants into the drawing-room every morning to give them their orders for the day. 'I believe in keeping up home standards,' said Désirée, whose parents were hotel managers. Sybil was not sure where Désirée had got the idea of herding all the domestics into her presence each morning. Perhaps it was some family-prayer assembly in her ancestral memory, or possibly it had been some hotel-staff custom which prompted her to 'have in the servants' and instruct them beyond their capacity. These half-domesticated peasants and erstwhile small-farmers stood, bare-footed and woolly-cropped, in clumsy postures on Désirée's carpet. In pidgin dialect which they largely failed to comprehend, she enunciated the duties of each one. Only Sybil and David Carter knew that the natives' name for Désirée was, translated, 'Bad Hen'. Désirée complained much about their stupidity, but she enjoyed this morning palaver as Barry relished his poetry.

'Carter writes poetry too,' said Barry with a laugh one day.

Désirée shrieked. 'Poetry! Oh, Barry, you can't call that stuff *poetry*.'

'It is frightful,' Barry said, 'but the poor fellow doesn't know it.'

'I should like to see it,' Sybil said.

'You aren't interested in Carter by any chance, Sybil?' said Désirée.

'How do you mean?'

'Personally, I mean.'

'Well, I think he's all right.'

'Be honest, Sybil,' said Barry. Sybil felt extremely irritated. He so often appealed for frankness in others, as if by right; was so dishonest with himself. 'Be honest, Sybil – you're after David Carter.'

'He's handsome,' Sybil said.

'You haven't a chance,' said Barry. 'He's mad keen on Désirée. And anyway, Sybil, you don't want a beginner.'

'You want a mature man in a good position,' said Désirée. 'The life you're living isn't natural for a girl. I've been noticing,' she said, 'you and Carter being matey together out on the farm.'

Towards the end of her stay David Carter produced his verses 55 for Sybil to read. She thought them interesting but unpractised. She told him so, and was disappointed that he did not take this as a reasonable criticism. He was very angry. 'Of course,' she said, 'your poetry is far better than Barry's.' This failed to appease David. After a while, when she was meeting him in the town where she lived, she began to praise his poems, persuading herself that he was fairly talented.

She met him whenever he could get away. She sent excuses in answer to Désirée's pressing invitations. For different reasons, both Sybil and David were anxious to keep their meetings secret from the Westons. Sybil did not want the affair mythologized and gossiped about. For David's part, he valued his job in the flourishing passion-fruit concern. He had confided to Sybil his hope, one day, to have the whole business under his control. He might even buy Barry out. 'I know far more about it than he does. He's getting more and more bound up with his poetry, and paying next to no attention to the business. I'm just waiting.' He is, Sybil remarked to herself on hearing this, a true poet all right.

David reported that the quarrels between Désirée and Barry were becoming more violent, that the possibility of Barry's resigning from business to devote his time to poetry was haunting Désirée. 'Why don't you come,' Désirée wrote, 'and talk to Barry about his poetry? Why don't you come and see us now? What have we done? Poor Sybil, all alone in the world, you ought to be married. David Carter follows me all over the place, it's most embarrassing, you know how furious Barry gets. Well, I suppose that's the cost of having a devoted husband.' Perhaps, thought Sybil, she senses that David is my lover.

One day she went down with flu. David turned up unexpectedly and proposed marriage. He clung to her with violent, large hands. She alone, he said, understood his ambitions, his art, himself. Within a year or two they could, together, take over the passion-fruit plantation.

'Sh-sh, Ariadne will hear you.' Ariadne was out, in fact. David looked at her somewhat wildly. 'We must be married,' he said.

Sybil's affair with David Carter was over, from her point of view, almost before it had started. She had engaged in it as an act of virtue done against the grain, and for a brief time it had absolved her from the reproach of her sexlessness.

'I'm waiting for an answer.' By his tone, he seemed to suspect what the answer would be.

'Oh, David, I was just about to write to you. We really must put an end to this. As for marriage, well, I'm not cut out for it at all.'

He stooped over her bed and clung to her. 'You'll catch my flu,' she said. 'I'll think about it,' she said, to get rid of him.

When he had gone she wrote him her letter, sipping lemon juice to ease her throat. She noticed he had brought for her, and left on the floor of the stoep, six bottles of Weston's Passion-fruit Juice. He will soon get over the affair, she thought, he has still got his obsession with the passion-fruit business.

But in response to her letter David forced his way into the house. Sybil was alarmed. None of her previous lovers had persisted in this way.

'It's your duty to marry me.'

'Really, what next?'

'It's your duty to me as a man and a poet.' She did not like his eyes.

'As a poet,' she said, 'I think you're a third-rater.' She felt relieved to hear her own voice uttering the words.

He stiffened up in a comical melodramatic style, looking such a clean-cut settler with his golden hair and tropical suiting.

'David Carter,' wrote Désirée, 'has gone on the bottle. I think he's bats, myself. It's because I keep giving him the brush-off. Isn't it all silly? The estate will go to ruin if Barry doesn't get rid of him. Barry has sent him away on leave for a month, but if he hasn't improved on his return we shall have to make a change. When are you coming? Barry needs to talk to you.'

Sybil went the following week, urged on by her old self-despising; driving her Ford V8 against the current of pleasure, yet compelled to expiate her abnormal nature by contact with the Westons' sexuality, which she knew, none the less, would bore her.

They twisted the knife within an hour of her arrival.

'Haven't you found a man yet?' said Barry.

'You ought to try a love affair,' said Désirée. 'We've been saying – haven't we, Barry? – you ought to, Sybil. It would be good for you. It isn't healthy, the life you lead. That's why you get flu so often. It's psychological.'

'Come out on the lawn,' Barry had said when she first arrived. 'We've got the ciné camera out. Come and be filmed.'

Désirée said, 'Carter came back this morning.'

'Oh, is he here? I thought he was away for a month.'

'So did we. But he turned up this morning.'

'He's moping,' Barry said, 'about Désirée. She snubs him so badly.'

'He's psychological,' said Désirée.

'I love that striped awning,' said Sybil's hostess. 'It puts the finishing touch on the whole scene. How carefree you all look – don't they, Ted?'

58

'*That* chap looks miserable,' Ted observed. He referred to a shot of David Carter who had just ambled within range of the camera.

Everyone laughed, for David looked exceedingly grim.

'He was caught in an off-moment there,' said Sybil's hostess. 'Oh, there goes Sybil. I thought you looked a little sad just then, Sybil. There's that other girl again, and the lovely dog.'

'Was this a *typical* afternoon in the Colony?' inquired the young man.

'It was and it wasn't,' Sybil said.

Whenever they had the camera out life changed at the Westons'. Everyone, including the children, had to look very happy. The house natives were arranged to appear in the background wearing their best whites. Sometimes Barry would have everyone dancing in a ring with the children, and the natives had to clap time.

Or, as on the last occasion, he would stage an effect of gracious living. The head cook-boy, who had a good knowledge of photography, was placed at his post.

'Ready,' said Barry to the cook, 'shoot.'

Désirée came out, followed by the dog.

'Look frisky, Barker,' said Barry. The Alsatian looked frisky.

Barry put one arm round Désirée and his other arm through Sybil's that late afternoon, walking them slowly across the camera range. He chatted with amiability and with an actor's lift of the head. He would accentuate his laughter, tossing back his head. A sound track would, however, have reproduced the words, 'Smile, Sybil. Walk slowly. Look as if you're enjoying it. You'll be able to see yourself in later years having the time of your life.'

Sybil giggled.

Just then David was seen to be securing the little lake boat between the trees, 'He must have come across the lake,' said Barry. 'I wonder if he's been drinking again?'

But David's walk was quite steady. He did not realize he was being photographed as he crossed the long lawn. He stood for a moment staring at Sybil. She said, 'Oh, hallo, David.' He turned and walked aimlessly face-on towards the camera.

'Hold it a minute,' Barry called out to the cook.

The boy obeyed at the moment David realized he had been filmed.

'OK,' shouted Barry, when David was out of range. 'Fire ahead.'

It was then Barry said to Sybil, 'Haven't you found a man yet . . .?' and Désirée said, 'You ought to try a love affair . . .'

'We've made Sybil unhappy,' said Désirée.

'Oh, I'm quite happy.'

'Well, cheer up in front of the camera,' said Barry.

The sun was setting fast, the camera was folded away, and everyone had gone to change. Sybil came down and sat on the stoep outside the open french windows of the dining-room. Presently, Désirée was indoors behind her, adjusting the oil lamps which one of the houseboys had set too high. Désirée put her head round the glass door and remarked to Sybil, 'That Benjamin's a fool, I shall speak to him in the morning. He simply will not take care with these lamps. One day we'll have a real smoke-out.'

Sybil said, 'Oh, I expect they are all so used to electricity these days . . .'

'That's the trouble,' said Désirée, and turned back into the room.

Sybil was feeling disturbed by David's presence in the place.

She wondered if he would come in to dinner. Thinking of his sullen staring at her on the lawn, she felt he might make a scene. She heard a gasp from the dining-room behind her.

She looked round, but in the same second it was over. A deafening crack from the pistol and Désirée crumpled up. A movement by the inner door and David held the gun to his head. Sybil screamed, and was aware of running footsteps upstairs. The gun exploded again and David's body dropped sideways.

With Barry and the natives she went round to the dining-room. Désirée was dead. David lingered a moment enough to roll his eyes in Sybil's direction as she rose from Désirée's body. He knows, thought Sybil quite lucidly, that he got the wrong woman.

'What I can't understand,' said Barry when he called on Sybil a few weeks later, 'is why he did it.'

'He was mad,' said Sybil.

'Not all that mad,' said Barry. 'And everyone thinks, of course that there was an affair between them. That's what I can't bear.'

'Quite,' said Sybil. 'But of course he was keen on Désirée. You always said so. Those rows you used to have . . . You always made out you were jealous of David.'

'Do you know,' he said, 'I wasn't, really. It was a sort of . . . a sort of . . .'

'Play-act,' said Sybil.

'Sort of. You see, there was nothing between them,' he said. 'And honestly, Carter wasn't a bit interested in Désirée. And the question is *why* he did it. I can't bear people to think . . .'

The damage to his pride, Sybil saw, outweighed his grief. The sun was setting and she rose to put on the stoep light.

'Stop!' he said. 'Turn round. My God, you did look like Désirée for a moment.'

'You're nervy,' she said, and switched on the light.

'In some ways you *do* look a little like Désirée,' he said. 'In some lights,' he said reflectively.

I must say something, thought Sybil, to blot this notion from his mind. I must make this occasion unmemorable, distasteful to him.

'At all events,' she said, 'you've still got your poetry.'

'That's the great thing,' he said, 'I've still got that. It means everything to me, a great consolation. I'm selling up the estate and joining up. The kids are going into a convent and I'm going up north. What we need is some good war poetry. There hasn't been any war poetry.'

'You'll make a better soldier,' she said, 'than a poet.'

'What do you say?'

She repeated her words fairly slowly, and with a sense of relief, almost of absolution. The season of falsity had formed a scab, soon to fall away altogether. There is no health, she thought, for me, outside of honesty.

'You've always,' he said, 'thought my poetry was wonderful.'

'I have said so.' she said, 'but it was a sort of play-act. Of course, it's only my opinion, but I think you're a third-rate poet.'

'You're upset, my dear,' he said.

He sent her the four reels of film from Cairo a month before he was killed in action. 'It will be nice in later years,' he wrote, 'for you to recall those good times we used to have.'

'It has been delightful,' said her hostess. 'You haven't changed a bit. Do you *feel* any different?'

'Well yes, I feel rather differently about everything, of course.' One learns to accept oneself.

'A hundred feet of one's past life!' said the young man. 'If they were mine, I'm sure I should be shattered. I should be calling, "Lights! Lights!" like Hamlet's uncle.'

Sybil smiled at him. He looked back, suddenly solemn and shrewd.

'How tragic, those people being killed in shooting affairs,' said the elderly woman.

'The last reel was the best,' said her hostess. 'The garden was entrancing. I should like to see that one again; what about you, Ted?'

'Yes, I liked those nature-study shots. I feel I missed a lot of it,' said her husband.

'Hark at him – nature-study shots!'

'Well, those close-ups of tropical plants.'

Everyone wanted the last one again.

'How about you, Sybil?'

Am I a woman, she thought calmly, or an intellectual monster? She was so accustomed to this question within herself that it needed no answer. She said, 'Yes, I should like to see it again. It's an interesting experience.'

The Seraph and the Zambesi

You may have heard of Samuel Cramer, half poet, half journalist, who had to do with a dancer called the Fanfarlo. But, as you will see, it doesn't matter if you have not. He was said to be going strong in Paris early in the nineteenth century, and when I met him in 1946 he was still going strong, but this time in a different way. He was the same man, but modified. For instance, in those days, more than a hundred years ago, Cramer had persisted for several decades, and without affectation, in being about twenty-five years old. But when I knew him he was clearly undergoing his forty-two-year-old phase.

At this time he was keeping a petrol pump some four miles south of the Zambesi River where it crashes over a precipice at the Victoria Falls. Cramer had some spare rooms where he put up visitors to the Falls when the hotel was full. I was sent to him because it was Christmas week and there was no room in the hotel.

I found him trying the starter of a large, lumpy Mercedes outside his corrugated-iron garage, and at first sight I judged him to be a Belgian from the Congo. He had the look of north and south, light hair with canvas-coloured skin. Later, however, he told me that his father was German and his mother Chilean. It was this information rather than the 'S. Cramer' above the garage door which made me think I had heard of him.

The rains had been very poor and that December was fiercely hot. On the third night before Christmas I sat on the stoep outside my room, looking through the broken mosquito-wire network at the lightning in the distance. When an atmosphere maintains an excessive temperature for a long spell something seems to happen to the natural noises of life. Sound fails to carry in its usual quantity, but comes as if bound and gagged. That night the Christmas beetles, which fall on their backs on every stoep with a high tic-tac, seemed to be shock-absorbed. I saw one fall and the little bump reached my ears a fraction behind time. The noises of minor wild beasts from the bush were all hushed-up, too. In fact it wasn't until the bush noises all stopped simultaneously, as they frequently do when a leopard is about, that I knew there had been any sound at all.

Overlying this general muted hum, Cramer's sundowner party progressed farther up the stoep. The heat distorted every word. The glasses made a tinkle that was not of the substance of glass, but of bottles wrapped in tissue paper. Sometimes, for a moment, a shriek or a cackle would hang torpidly in space, but these were unreal sounds, as if projected from a distant country, as if they were pocket-torches seen through a London fog.

Cramer came over to my end of the stoep and asked me to join his party. I said I would be glad to, and meant it, even though I had been glad to sit alone. Heat so persistent and so intense sucks up the will.

Five people sat in wicker arm-chairs drinking highballs and chewing salted peanuts. I recognized a red-haired trooper from Livingstone, just out from England, and two of Cramer's lodgers, a tobacco planter and his wife from Bulawayo. In the custom of those parts, the other two were introduced by their first names. Mannie, a short dark man of square face and build, I thought might be a Portuguese from the east coast. The woman, Fanny, was picking bits out of the frayed wicker chair and as she lifted her glass her hand shook a little, making her bracelets chime. 65

She would be about fifty, a well-tended woman, very neat. Her grey hair, tinted with blue, was done in a fringe above a face puckered with malaria.

In the general way of passing the time with strangers in that countryside, I exchanged with the tobacco people the names of acquaintances who lived within a six-hundred-mile radius of where we sat, reducing this list to names mutually known to us. The trooper contributed his news from the region between Lusaka and Livingstone. Meanwhile an argument was in process between Cramer, Fanny and Mannie, of which Fanny seemed to be getting the better. It appeared there was to be a play or concert on Christmas Eve in which the three were taking part. I several times heard the words 'troupe of angels', 'shepherds', 'ridiculous price' and 'my girls' which seemed to be key words in the argument. Suddenly, on hearing the trooper mention a name, Fanny broke off her talk and turned to us.

'She was one of my girls,' she said, 'I gave her lessons for three years.'

Mannie rose to leave, and before Fanny followed him she picked a card from her handbag and held it out to me between her finger nails.

'If any of your friends are interested . . .' said Fanny hazily.

I looked at this as she drove off with the man, and above an address about four miles up the river I read:

> Mme La Fanfarlo (Paris, London)
> Dancing Instructress. Ballet. Ballroom.
> Transport provided By Arrangement

Next day I came across Cramer still trying to locate the trouble with the Mercedes.

'Are you the man Baudelaire wrote about?' I asked him.

He stared past me at the open waste veldt with a look of tried patience.

'Yes,' he replied. 'What made you think of it?'

'The name Fanfarlo on Fanny's card,' I said. 'Didn't you know her in Paris?'

'Oh, yes,' said Cramer, 'but those days are finished. She married Manuela de Monteverde – that's Mannie. They settled here about twenty years ago. He keeps a Kaffir store.'

I remembered then that in the Romantic age it had pleased Cramer to fluctuate between the practice of verse and that of belles-lettres, together with the living up to such practices.

I asked him, 'Have you given up your literary career?'

'*As* a career, yes,' he answered. 'It was an obsession I was glad to get rid of.'

He stroked the blunt bonnet of the Mercedes and added, 'The greatest literature is the occasional kind, a mere afterthought.'

Again he looked across the veldt where, unseen, a grey-crested lourie was piping 'go'way, go'way'.

'Life,' Cramer continued, 'is the important thing.'

'And do you write occasional verses?' I inquired.

'When occasion demands it,' he said. 'In fact I've just written a Nativity Masque. We're giving a performance on Christmas Eve in there.' He pointed to his garage, where a few natives were already beginning to shift petrol cans and tyres. Being members neither of the cast nor the audience, they were taking their time. A pile of folded seats had been dumped alongside.

Late on the morning of Christmas Eve I returned from the Falls to find a crowd of natives quarrelling outside the garage, with Cramer swearing loud and heavy in the middle. He held a sulky man by the shirt-sleeve, while with the other hand he described his vituperation on the hot air. Some mission natives had been sent over to give a hand with laying the stage, and these, with their standard-three school English, washed faces and white drill shorts, had innocently provoked Cramer's raw rag-dressed boys. Cramer's method, which ended with the word 'police', succeeded in sending them back to work, still uttering drum-like gutturals at each other.

The stage, made of packing-cases with planks nailed across, was being put at the back of the building, where a door led to the yard, the privy and the native huts. The space between this door and the stage was closed off by a row of black Government blankets hung on a line; this was to be the dressing-room. I agreed to come round there that evening to help with the lighting, the make-up, and the pinning on of angels' wings. The Fanfarlo's dancing pupils were to make an angel chorus with carols and dancing, while she herself, as the Virgin, was to give a representative ballet performance. Owing to her husband's very broken English, he had been given a silent role as a shepherd, supported by three other shepherds chosen for like reasons. Cramer's part was the most prominent, for he had the longest speeches, being the First Seraph. It had been agreed that, since he had written the masque, he could best deliver most of it; but I gathered there had been some trouble at rehearsals over the cost of the production, with Fanny wanting elaborate scenery as being due to her girls.

The performance was set to begin at eight. I arrived behind the stage at seven fifteen to find the angels assembled in ballet dresses with wings of crinkled paper in various shades. The Fanfarlo wore a long white transparent skirt with a sequin top. I was helping to fix on the Wise Men's beards when I saw Cramer. He had on a toga-like garment made up of several thicknesses of mosquito-net, but not thick enough to hide his white shorts underneath. He had put on his make-up early, and this was melting on his face in the rising heat.

'I always get nerves at this point,' he said. 'I'm going to practise my opening speech.'

I heard him mount the stage and begin reciting. Above the voices of excited children I could only hear the rhythm of his voice; and I was intent on helping the Fanfarlo to paint her girls' faces. It seemed impossible. As fast as we lifted the sticks of paint they turned liquid. It was really getting abnormally hot.

'Open that door,' yelled the Fanfarlo. The back door was opened and a crowd of curious natives pressed round the entrance. I left the Fanfarlo ordering them off, for I was determined to get to the front of the building for some air. I mounted the stage and began to cross it when I was aware of a powerful radiation of heat coming from my right. Looking round, I saw Cramer apparently shouting at someone, in the attitude of his dealings with the natives that morning. But he could not advance because of this current of heat. And because of the heat I could not at first make out who Cramer was rowing with; this was the sort of heat that goes for the eyes. But as I got farther towards the front of the stage I saw what was standing there.

This was a living body. The most noticeable thing was its constancy; it seemed not to conform to the law of perspective, but remained the same size when I approached as when I withdrew. And altogether unlike other forms of life, it had a completed look. No part was undergoing a process; the outline lacked the signs of confusion and ferment which are commonly the signs of living things, and this was also the principle of its beauty. The eyes took up nearly the whole of the head, extending far over the cheekbones. From the back of the head came two muscular wings which from time to time folded themselves over the eyes, making a draught of scorching air. There was hardly any neck. Another pair of wings, tough and supple, spread from below the shoulders, and a third pair extended from the calves of the legs, appearing to sustain the body. The feet looked too fragile to bear up such a concentrated degree of being.

European residents of Africa are often irresistibly prompted to speak kitchen kaffir to anything strange.

'*Hamba!*' shouted Cramer, meaning 'Go away'.

'Now get off the stage and stop your noise,' said the living body peaceably.

'Who in hell are you?' said Cramer, gasping through the heat.

'The same as in Heaven,' came the reply, 'a Seraph, that's to say.'

'Tell that to someone else,' Cramer panted. 'Do I look like a fool?'

'I will. No, nor a Seraph either,' said the Seraph.

The place was filling with heat from the Seraph. Cramer's paint was running into his eyes and he wiped them on his net robe. Walking backward to a less hot place he cried, 'Once and for all –'

'That's correct,' said the Seraph.

'– this is my show,' continued Cramer.

'Since when?' the Seraph said.

'Right from the start,' Cramer breathed at him.

'Well, it's been mine from the Beginning,' said the Seraph, 'and the Beginning began first.'

Climbing down from the hot stage, Cramer caught his seraphic robe on a nail and tore it. 'Listen here,' he said, 'I can't conceive of an abnormality like you being a true Seraph.'

70   'True,' said the Seraph.

By this time I had been driven by the heat to the front entrance. Cramer joined me there. A number of natives had assembled. The audience had begun to arrive in cars and the rest of the cast had come round the building from the back. It was impossible to see far inside the building owing to the Seraph's heat, and impossible to re-enter.

Cramer was still haranguing the Seraph from the door, and there was much speculation among the new arrivals as to which of the three familiar categories the present trouble came under, namely, the natives, Whitehall, or leopards.

'This is my property,' cried Cramer, 'and these people have paid for their seats. They've come to see a masque.'

'In that case,' said the Seraph, 'I'll cool down and they can come and see a masque.'

'*My* masque,' said Cramer.

'Ah, no, *mine*,' said the Seraph. 'Yours won't do.'

'Will you go, or shall I call the police?' said Cramer with finality.

'I have no alternative,' said the Seraph more finally still.

Word had gone round that a mad leopard was in the garage. People got back into their cars and parked at a safe distance; the tobacco planter went to fetch a gun. A number of young troopers had the idea of blinding the mad leopard with petrol and ganged up some natives to fill petrol cans from the pump and pass them chainwise to the garage.

'This'll fix him,' said a trooper.

'That's right, let him have it,' said Cramer from his place by the door.

'I shouldn't do that,' said the Seraph. 'You'll cause a fire.'

The first lot of petrol to be flung into the heat flared up. The seats caught alight first, then the air itself began to burn within the metal walls till the whole interior was flame feeding on flame. Another car-load of troopers arrived just then and promptly got a gang of natives to fill petrol cans with water. Slowly they drenched the fire. The Fanfarlo mustered her angels a little way up the road. She was trying to reassure their parents and see what was happening at the same time, furious at losing her opportunity to dance. She aimed a hard poke at the back of one of the angels whose parents were in England.

It was some hours before the fire was put out. While the corrugated metal walls still glowed, twisted and furled, it was impossible to see what had happened to the Seraph, and after they had ceased to glow it was too dark and hot to see far into the wreck.

'Are you insured?' one of Cramer's friends asked him.

'Oh, yes,' Cramer replied, 'my policy covers everything except Acts of God – that means lightning or flood.'

'He's fully covered,' said Cramer's friend to another friend.

Many people had gone home and the rest were going. The troopers drove off singing 'Good King Wenceslas', and the mission boys ran down the road singing 'Good Christian Men, Rejoice'.

It was about midnight, and still very hot. The tobacco planters suggested a drive to the Falls, where it was cool. Cramer and the Fanfarlo joined us, and we bumped along the rough path from Cramer's to the main highway. There the road is tarred only in two strips to take car-wheels. The thunder of the Falls reached us about two miles before we reached them.

'After all my work on the masque and everything!' Cramer was saying.

'Oh, shut up,' said the Fanfarlo.

72   Just then, by the glare of our headlights I saw the Seraph

again, going at about seventy miles an hour and skimming the tarmac strips with two of his six wings in swift motion, two folded over his face, and two covering his feet.

'That's him!' said Cramer. 'We'll get him yet.'

We left the car near the hotel and followed a track through the dense vegetation of the Rain Forest, where the spray from the Falls descends perpetually. It was like a convalescence after fever, that frail rain after the heat. The Seraph was far ahead of us and through the trees I could see where his heat was making steam of the spray.

We came to the cliff's edge, where opposite us and from the same level the full weight of the river came blasting into the gorge between. There was no sign of the Seraph. Was he far below in the heaving pit, or where?

Then I noticed that along the whole mile of the waterfall's crest the spray was rising higher than usual. This I took to be steam from the Seraph's heat. I was right, for presently, by the mute flashes of summer lightning, we watched him ride the Zambesi away from us, among the rocks that look like crocodiles and the crocodiles that look like rocks.

The Dragon

I was standing talking at a cocktail party when I was saddened to see that everybody formed a forest. I felt defeated. The Dragon had taken over.

No sooner did I feel this, than I decided it was only a temporary defeat, for that is what I am like. I didn't see then how I could possibly do it, but certainly, I decided, I was going to stop the Dragon. The party was people again. I picked up the conversation at the point where a man in the group was talking. He was good-looking, about sixty. 'My address book,' he was saying, 'is becoming like a necropolis, so many people dying every month, this friend, that friend. You have to draw a line through their names. It's very sad.' 'I always use pencil,' said a lady, a little younger, 'then when people pass on I can rub them out.'

We were in a shady part of the garden. It was six o'clock on a hot evening in the north of Italy. It was my garden, my party. The Dragon came oozing through the foliage. She was holding her drink, a Pimm's No. 1, and was followed by a tall, strikingly handsome truck-driver whom she had brought along to the party on the spur of the moment. To her dismay, discernible only to myself, he was a genial, easy-mannered young man, rather amused to be taking half-an-hour off the job with his truck parked outside the gate. I knew very well that when she had picked him up at the bar across the street she had hoped he would be an embarrassment, a nuisance.

Oh, the Dragon! Dragon was what it was her job to be. She

had been highly and pressingly recommended by one of my clients, the widow of a well-known dramatist. It didn't occur to me, then, that the vertiginous blurb that was written to me about the girl was in fact so excessive as to be suspicious. Perhaps I did feel uneasy about the eulogies that came over the telephone, and the letters which the widow wrote to me from Gstaad about the Dragon and her virtues as such. Perhaps I did. But, as often when I want to believe something enough because I am in need of help, I didn't listen to the small inner voice which said, Something is wrong, or which said, Be careful. I was optimistic and enthusiastic.

I was first and foremost a needlewoman. I have been called a *couturier*, a dressmaker, a designer. But it was my fascination with the needle and thread that earned me my reputation. I could have gone into big business, I could have merged with any of the world's famous houses of *haute couture*. But I would have none of that. I preferred to keep my own exclusive and small clientele. It wasn't everybody I would sew for.

When I left school at the beginning of the sixties there were two things I could do well. One was write a good letter in fine calligraphy, and the other was sew, by hand, with every stitch perfect. I worked as a seamstress, in the alterations department of a London store. This taught me a lot, but it didn't satisfy me. At home, I started making my own clothes. I had learned at my evening classes how to make an individual working dummy for each client. I was very careful about this, and I practised on my grandmother with whom I lived. You cut a length of buckram into a body-shape and sew your lady into it over the minimum of underwear. I did this with my grandmother, basting the buckram on her body with only an exact inch to spare. She thought she would never get out of it again. Then, I slit it up the front with my scissors, sewed it up again the exact one-inch seam. When I had perfected the sewing on the buckram with even, small, back-stitching I filled the shape with fine-teased raw wool. There was my grandmother's perfect shape to set on my stand. Some dressmakers use synthetic fabrics, if they still employ this process, but I wouldn't touch them.

I made my grandmother a dress she was proud of to the day she died. It was velvet lined with silk, every inside-seam edged with narrow lace, both dress and lining. Nobody could see how beautifully it was finished inside. I have always stitched lace to my inside seams. Even if nobody ever saw the reverse side, my clients were the sort of women who are satisfied with the knowledge that they are beautifully dressed in garments made by hand and edged inside with very narrow lace, even when a silk lining hides the whip-stitched lace-edged seams. Hem-stitch, back-stitch, cross-stitch, slip-stitch, buttonhole stitch – I can do them to perfection. No sewing machine has ever stood in my workshop. You might say it was my obsession to turn out a hand-made dress. My clients would say, 'Do you mean that you even do the long seams by hand?' 'Everything by hand,' I replied. It's been the secret of my success. You would be surprised at the demand for dresses and blouses and skirts and underwear all made by hand – I've accomplished entire *trousseaux* for clients who were prepared to give me time and pay the price.

A long time has passed since I made my grandmother's dress, and since I set up on my own. My reputation as a superb seamstress was growing all the time, so that I no longer made clothes from paper patterns but employed my own men as cutters and designers. For cutting and designing you can't beat a man; and the clients prefer them, too. The cutters and designers have come and gone over the years. I never married any of them although I came near to doing so very often. Something within me told me not to make a permanent life with any of the cutters and designers. Fashions change so much from season to season, year to year. Cutters and designers often get stuck in a certain period, and never move on; their best work is over. Needleworkers, on the other hand, never go out of date, and I was always a needlewoman with a difference. There is a big difference between the seams that are right for velvet and those for chiffon, and I have devised ways of sewing a lace dress where you wouldn't know there was any seam at all. Lately I got my needles from Frankfurt, and my threads from London. My speciality was in the textiles that I obtained from all over the world.

So I had come to Como for silk, and was already fairly comfortably placed with my exclusive clientele. Like my textiles, they came from all parts of the world, even the wives of ambassadors from Eastern Europe. I saw a lovely house for sale on the shores of Lake Como and decided to settle there, and make a new workshop.

Now I was so well known for my hand-made dresses that I had to have some sort of protection. It takes a long time to make one hand-made evening dress or wedding-gown, so I couldn't possibly answer the telephone to all the millionairesses and their secretaries, who wanted me to work for them. Ordinary maids and *au pair* helpers were very weak, and easily bribed. They would let people in or call me to the phone just when I was stitching a circular piece or a corner – very much precision-work. My temperament wouldn't stand it. At the same time, I had learned over the years that the more you discourage your prospective clients the more they want your work, and the higher the price they are prepared to pay.

I decided to take on a Dragon, whose job it was to keep new

clients at a distance, to tell them that they must write for an appointment; and she was to be very firm about this. Her other job was to look after the files of all my clients of the past, so that my business could go forward in good order, with that personal touch of remembering small items when the client finally succeeded in making an appointment. At this time I had a brilliant cutter called Daniele; he couldn't design originals, but that is a small matter; Daniele could copy and adapt. I would advise him a little – which materials to cut on the bias and which to cut, for instance, with the patterns not matching at the seams, to make an intriguing change. I usually did the fittings and pinnings myself, because I have that very exact eye. Daniele was well-paid. He was inclined to be arrogant; he felt the traditional *couture* business, where the designers employ the cutters and seamstresses, was the true thing, and that my method was the wrong way round. But I soon let him know how to mind his business, and the pay kept him quiet.

I started to interview Dragons. A sewing assistant, I explained, was out of the question for me. All the more did I need protection, and time, long stretches of time all to myself. Every stitch had to be perfect, I explained, small and perfect. Even the basting and tacking stitches, which later had to be drawn out, had to be done by me, or I could not sleep at night. Sometimes, to make an elaborate dress, I needed two clear months, working on that one dress alone. With embroidery, I needed three or four months. All this I explained to the candidates for the job. There were eight. I brought them out from England to be interviewed on the spot where the job was offered. A frightened bunch, with one exception. The others were glad to get away after the interview and profit by their trip to Italy to go and see the sights and have a good time. The eighth looked more suspicious than afraid while I explained what the job was to be. She frowned a lot. Emily Butler. Tall, skinny, with her top teeth protruding, and a lot of red hair. She understood a little Italian and spoke French, as indeed had the other girls whom I'd brought out to be interviewed, otherwise I wouldn't have brought them. But Emily: I thought she would make a good Dragon. She was to keep everybody away from me except an approved short list of clients, or people highly recommended by the clients. Even then, I was never to be called to the telephone. The client must either write or leave a number for me to call back at my leisure. Emily had brought an additional good reference from an opera singer she had worked for; she seemed to understand what was wanted, I remembered having heard somewhere that women with protruding teeth are very attractive to men, but I didn't see that this was a factor that mattered, anyway. In fact, what happened had nothing to do with Emily's teeth.

The Dragon was a marvel that spring and early summer. I worked without a break, seven days a week, sometimes twelve hours a day, frequently in a summer-house in the garden except during the very hot hours of the day when I kept to my air-conditioned workroom. I must tell you about the garden and about the house.

The house was set well back from the road on a high cliff looking over the lake. It had been built at the turn of the century with many features of *art-nouveau*, such as stained-glass windows, curly banisters, and fruity decorations above the doors. From the outside, the villa seemed to have more colonnades, arches, terraces, bow-windows and turrets than its size really warranted; this means, for instance, that there were two turrets, and one would have been enough. The garden was large, really out of proportion to the house; but this suited me very well. I liked to sit and sew in the garden, especially under a mighty cedar tree that had become my banner; you could see it from the opposite shore of the lake, you could look down on it from the cliff-road; wherever you were, or from wherever you approached in those parts you couldn't miss the cedar tree. It soared above the statues in the garden. There, on the garden seat I would do my buttonholing in tranquillity – for I would never sew a zip fastener into a dress – looping the thread as I made each stitch; and if it was a blouse to be embroidered I used to sit coolly and do my satin-stitch or split-stitch.

In the garden were white stone statues of the period. They represented the Four Seasons and Four Arts (Painting, Sculpture, Music and Literature). The Seasons were female figures and the Arts, male, but all garbed so that it made very little difference. The Painter held a palette in one hand and a paintbrush in the other; the Sculptor worked on a stone lion; the Musician held a flute in his left hand, with his arm stretched out, and with the other, corrected a music score that was cleverly set up in stone in front of him; the Writer reclined, making notes in a book. The Seasons were garlanded according to the time of year they represented; their hair flowed; Winter was adorned with holly and icicles; Spring with flowers of the field; Summer with roses and cherries; Autumn had a necklace of grapes, and leaned on a sheaf of corn. The garden was very striking. Some of my clients would exclaim over it, with delight; others would just stare and, with a strange silence, say nothing at all. As for the statues, they struck me as odd sometimes when I turned suddenly and looked back at them. They looked exactly the same as before; that is, they seemed to have recomposed their features. What had been their expression behind my back?

The Dragon erupted in her spare time with Daniele the

cutter, and they made love after lunch in the room off the cool back kitchen where the Dragon slept. Her red hair was growing longer and she kept it flying loose. She said it was Pre-Raphaelite, to go with the house.

In August came extraordinary rains, leaving the air between downfalls soporific and bewildered. The Dragon said to me, 'Why do you work so hard? What is it all for?' Nobody had ever before asked me a question like that. It seemed sacrilegious. I began to notice that my clients arrived late for their fittings. When you live out of town, you must expect certain delays. But, in fact they didn't come so very late to the house; rather, they were kept gossiping with the Dragon in her office, no matter that I was kept waiting in my workroom. Later, she wouldn't tell me what my clients had to say to her or she to them. I noticed that, with me, curiously enough, people started to speak in a low careful voice after they had first talked to the Dragon. When the Dragon took a boat out on the lake with Daniele, her red hair blew over her face; mostly, she came back drenched from the rain. Now, one day, I observed that she was breathing fire.

'Emily,' I said, 'I think you're not very well.'

'Can you wonder?' she said; and the smoke rose from her nostrils, flaming like her hair. 'Can you wonder? Always no, no, no on the telephone. Always, keep away, nobody come here, Madam is busy, have you an appointment? It wears you down,' she said, 'always playing the negative role.' Her nose was perfectly cool by now as if there had been no smoke, no flame flaring.

I agreed to let her invite the local people for an evening party. She brought a group from the smart hotel across the lake whom she had somehow got friendly with. She brought a number of Spaniards who were touring the lake, to make Daniele happy, 81 and Daniele's sister from Milan also arrived. I noticed that three of my most exclusive clients were among the women who came to that party. And there was the handsome truck-driver. The Dragon had called in a caterer of the first importance and ordered refreshments of the last rarity. She was efficient.

The Dragon had taken over, and I knew it when the forest formed around me. She came through the people, the trees, towards me, blowing fire. Then I saw that the statues, the Four Seasons, the Four Artists, were wearing materials from my workroom. They were pinned and draped as if the statues were my working manikins, and my guests marvelled at them. One of the statues, the Winter one, was actually wearing an evening dress that I was in the process of sewing. I looked round for Daniele. He was entertaining the boat-officer from the little lake port by blowing smoke through two cigarettes stuck one in each of his nostrils. The Dragon was drinking her Pimm's, green-eyed, watching me. I went up to the good-looking truck-driver who was standing around not knowing what to do with himself, and I said, 'Where are you going with your truck?' He was going to Düsseldorf with a load, and back again across Europe. His name was Simon K. Clegg, the 'K' standing for Kurt. For a few moments we discussed the adventures of heavy transport in the Common Market. Finally, I said, 'Let's go.'

I left the party and climbed into the truck beside him and off we went. Suddenly I remembered my raincoat and my passport, the two indispensable vade-mecums of travel, but Simon Kurt said, for a raincoat and a passport leave it to him. The Dragon ran up the road after us a little way, snorting and breathing green fire from her mouth – perhaps it had a copper sulphate or copper chloride basis; I have heard that you can get a green flame from skilfully blowing green Chartreuse on to a lighted candle. She was followed by Daniele. However, off we went, waving, leaving the Dragon and Daniele and the party and all my household to sort out the mess and the anxiety, and the stitching and matching, forever.

Forever? Before we reached the city of Como, nearly twenty-five miles from my house, my conversation with Simon K. Clegg had turned on the meaning of forever. We parked the truck and went for a walk into town to a bar where we ordered coffee and ice-creams. Simon said he definitely felt that he didn't understand 'forever', and doubted if there was any such thing as always and always, if that's what it meant. I told him that so far as I knew to date, forever was slip-stitch, split-stitch, cross-stitch, back-stitch; and also buttonhole and running-stitches.

'You've got me guessing,' said Simon. 'It's above my head, all that. Don't you want a lift, then? Get away from the party and all?'

I explained that the Dragon was in my home, questioning the value of all the materials and the sewing, the buckram, the soft, soft silk; and the run-and-fell seams, the fine lace edging. Button-holes. Satin-stitch. I told him about her liaison with Daniele the cutter.

'Her what?'

'Her love affair.'

'They should go away on holiday,' was Simon's point of view.

'There's too much work to do.'

'Well, if she's the lady in charge, it's up to her what she does in business hours. The garment industry's flourishing.'

'I am the lady in charge,' I said.

He was taken aback, as if he had been deceived.

'I thought,' he said, 'that you were some sort of employee.'

Really, he was a nice-looking truck-driver. He pushed away his glass of ice-cream as if he had something newly on his mind.

He said, 'My sister works in a textile and garment factory in Lyons. Good pay, short hours. She's a seamer.'

'A seamstress,' I said.

'She calls it seamer.'

'I sew my seams by hand,' I said.

'By hand? How do you do that?'

'With a needle and thread.'

'What does that involve?' he said, in a way that forced me to realize he had never seen a needle and thread.

I explained the technique of how you use the fingers of your right hand to replace the needle and shuttle of the sewing machine, while holding the material with your left hand. He listened carefully. He was almost deferential. 'It must save you a lot of electricity,' he observed.

'But surely,' I said, 'you've seen someone sewing on a button?'

'I don't have any clothes with buttons. Not in my line.'

But he was thinking of something else.

'Would you mind lying low in the cabin of the truck while I pass the customs and immigration?' he said. 'It's quite comfortable and they won't look in there. They just look at my papers. I've delivered half my load and I've got to take the rest across the St Gotthard to a hotel at Brunnen in Switzerland. Then on to Düsseldorf. Health crackers from Lyons.'

But I, too, was thinking of something else, and I didn't answer immediately.

'I thought you were an employee,' he said. 'If I'd known you were the employer I'd have thought up something better.'

It saddened me to hear the anxiety in his voice. I said, 'I'm afraid I'm in charge of my business.' I was thinking of the orders mounting up for next winter. I had a lady from Boston who was coming specially next Tuesday across the Atlantic, across the Alps, to order her dresses from my range of winter fabrics which included a length of wool so soft you would think it was muslin, coloured pale shrimp, and I had that deep blue silk-velvet, not quite midnight blue, but something like midnight with a glisten of royal blue which I would line with identical coloured silk, for an evening occasion, with the quarter-centimetre wide lace hand-sewn on all the seams. I had another client from Milan for my grey wool-chiffon with the almost indiscernible orange stripe, to be made up as a three-piece garment flowing like a wintry cloud; I had the design ready for the cutter and I had matched all the threads.

I was going on to think of other lengths and bales and clients when Simon penetrated my thoughts and ideas with his voice. 'Look, you're breathing fire. You must have some sort of electricity,' he said; and he stood up and took the check off the table. He looked shaken. 'I can see that you could be a Dragon in your way.'

I slipped out of the bar while he was paying the bill at the counter. I waited till after dark and hired a car to take me back to my villa. Everyone had gone home. The statues in the garden stood again unclothed. Emily Butler was in the living-room talking to Daniele. I had been sorry to part with the nice-looking truck-driver. He seemed to have a certain liking for me, a sympathy with my nature and my looks which I know are very much those of the serious unadorned seamstress. Some people like that sort of personality. But when I thought of how, as Simon had observed, I was really the Dragon in the case I couldn't have gone over the border with him. Perhaps forever. Neither my temperament nor my temperature would stand it.

I stood, now, at the living-room door and looked at Emily and Daniele. Emily gasped; Daniele sprang to his feet, his eyes terrified.

'She's breathing fire,' said Emily, and escaped through the french windows. Daniele followed her quickly, knocking over a chair as he went. He looked once over his shoulder, and then he was away after Emily.

I went to the kitchen and made some hot milk. I waited there while the sound of their creeping back, and the bumps of hasty packing went on in Daniele's room upstairs and Emily's at the back of the house.

Finally, they bundled themselves into the hall and out of the house, into Daniele's car, and away, without even waiting for their wages.

My business flourishes and I manage it without a Dragon. Without a cutter too, for I've found I have a talent for cutting. I've also invented a new stitch, the dragon-stitch. It looks lovely on the uneven hems of those dresses people like, which suggest the nineteen-thirties – for the evening but not too much. The essence of the dragon-stitch is that you see all the stitches; they are large, in a bright-coloured thick thread to contrast with the colour of the dress; one line and two forks, one line and two forks, in, out and away, all along the dipping and rising hemline, as if for always and always.

PENGUIN 60s

MARTIN AMIS · *God's Dice*
HANS CHRISTIAN ANDERSEN · *The Emperor's New Clothes*
MARCUS AURELIUS · *Meditations*
JAMES BALDWIN · *Sonny's Blues*
AMBROSE BIERCE · *An Occurrence at Owl Creek Bridge*
DIRK BOGARDE · *From Le Pigeonnier*
WILLIAM BOYD · *Killing Lizards*
POPPY Z. BRITE · *His Mouth will Taste of Wormwood*
ITALO CALVINO · *Ten Italian Folktales*
ALBERT CAMUS · *Summer*
TRUMAN CAPOTE · *First and Last*
RAYMOND CHANDLER · *Goldfish*
ANTON CHEKHOV · *The Black Monk*
ROALD DAHL · *Lamb to the Slaughter*
ELIZABETH DAVID · *I'll be with You in the Squeezing of a Lemon*
N. J. DAWOOD (TRANS.) · *The Seven Voyages of Sindbad the Sailor*
ISAK DINESEN · *The Dreaming Child*
SIR ARTHUR CONAN DOYLE · *The Man with the Twisted Lip*
DICK FRANCIS · *Racing Classics*
SIGMUND FREUD · *Five Lectures on Psycho-Analysis*
KAHLIL GIBRAN · *Prophet, Madman, Wanderer*
STEPHEN JAY GOULD · *Adam's Navel*
ALASDAIR GRAY · *Five Letters from an Eastern Empire*
GRAHAM GREENE · *Under the Garden*
JAMES HERRIOT · *Seven Yorkshire Tales*
PATRICIA HIGHSMITH · *Little Tales of Misogyny*
M. R. JAMES AND R. L. STEVENSON · *The Haunted Dolls' House*
RUDYARD KIPLING · *Baa Baa, Black Sheep*
PENELOPE LIVELY · *A Long Night at Abu Simbel*
KATHERINE MANSFIELD · *The Escape*

PENGUIN 60s

GABRIEL GARCÍA MÁRQUEZ · *Bon Voyage, Mr President*
PATRICK MCGRATH · *The Angel*
HERMAN MELVILLE · *Bartleby*
SPIKE MILLIGAN · *Gunner Milligan, 954024*
MICHEL DE MONTAIGNE · *Four Essays*
JAN MORRIS · *From the Four Corners*
JOHN MORTIMER · *Rumpole and the Younger Generation*
R. K. NARAYAN · *Tales from Malgudi*
ANAÏS NIN · *A Model*
FRANK O'CONNOR · *The Genius*
GEORGE ORWELL · *Pages from a Scullion's Diary*
CAMILLE PAGLIA · *Sex and Violence, or Nature and Art*
SARA PARETSKY · *A Taste of Life*
EDGAR ALLAN POE · *The Pit and the Pendulum*
MISS READ · *Village Christmas*
JEAN RHYS · *Let Them Call It Jazz*
DAMON RUNYON · *The Snatching of Bookie Bob*
SAKI · *The Secret Sin of Septimus Brope*
WILL SELF · *Scale*
GEORGES SIMENON · *Death of a Nobody*
MURIEL SPARK · *The Portobello Road*
ROBERT LOUIS STEVENSON · *The Pavilion on the Links*
PAUL THEROUX · *Down the Yangtze*
WILLIAM TREVOR · *Matilda's England*
MARK TULLY · *Ram Chander's Story*
JOHN UPDIKE · *Friends from Philadelphia*
EUDORA WELTY · *Why I Live at the P. O.*
EDITH WHARTON · *Madame de Treymes*
OSCAR WILDE · *The Happy Prince*
VIRGINIA WOOLF · *Killing the Angel in the House*

READ MORE IN PENGUIN

For complete information about books available from Penguin and how to order them, please write to us at the appropriate address below. Please note that for copyright reasons the selection of books varies from country to country.

IN THE UNITED KINGDOM: Please write to *Dept. JC, Penguin Books Ltd, FREEPOST, West Drayton, Middlesex UB7 OBR.*
If you have any difficulty in obtaining a title, please send your order with the correct money, plus ten per cent for postage and packaging, to *PO Box No. 11, West Drayton, Middlesex UB7 OBR.*

IN THE UNITED STATES: Please write to *Consumer Sales, Penguin USA, P.O. Box 999, Dept. 17109, Bergenfield, New Jersey 07621-0120.* VISA and MasterCard holders call 1-800-253-6476 to order all Penguin titles.

IN CANADA: Please write to *Penguin Books Canada Ltd, 10 Alcorn Avenue, Suite 300, Toronto, Ontario M4V 3B2.*

IN AUSTRALIA: Please write to *Penguin Books Australia Ltd, P.O. Box 257, Ringwood, Victoria 3134.*

IN NEW ZEALAND: Please write to *Penguin Books (NZ) Ltd, Private Bag 102902, North Shore Mail Centre, Auckland 10.*

IN INDIA: Please write to *Penguin Books India Pvt Ltd, 706 Eros Apartments, 56 Nehru Place, New Delhi 110 019.*

IN THE NETHERLANDS: Please write to *Penguin Books Netherlands bv, Postbus 3507, NL-1001 AH Amsterdam.*

IN GERMANY: Please write to *Penguin Books Deutschland GmbH, Metzlerstrasse 26, 60594 Frankfurt am Main.*

IN SPAIN: Please write to *Penguin Books S. A., Bravo Murillo 19, 1o B, 28015 Madrid.*

IN ITALY: Please write to *Penguin Italia s.r.l., Via Felice Casati 20, I-20124 Milano.*

IN FRANCE: Please write to *Penguin France S. A., 17 rue Lejeune, F-31000 Toulouse.*

IN JAPAN: Please write to *Penguin Books Japan, Ishikiribashi Building, 2-5-4, Suido, Bunkyo-ku, Tokyo 112.*

IN GREECE: Please write to *Penguin Hellas Ltd, Dimocritou 3, GR-106 71 Athens.*

IN SOUTH AFRICA: Please write to *Longman Penguin Southern Africa (Pty) Ltd, Private Bag X08, Bertsham 2013.*